Of The Bahamas

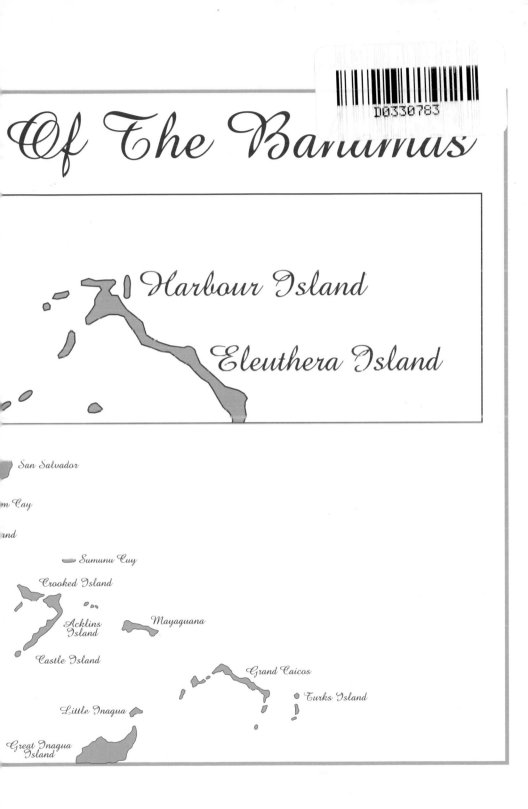

Harbour Island

Eleuthera Island

San Salvador

m Cay

and

Sumunu Cay

Crooked Island

Acklins Island

Mayaguana

Castle Island

Grand Caicos

Turks Island

Little Inagua

Great Inagua Island

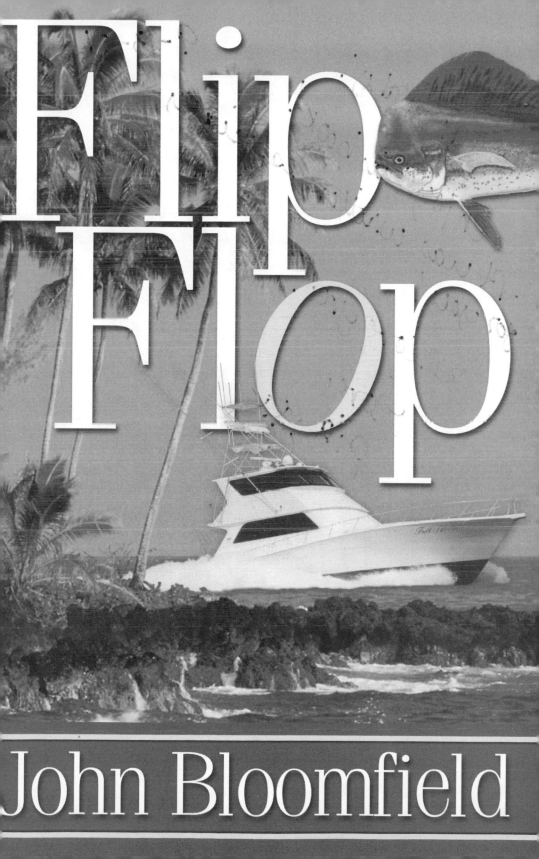

Flip
Flop

John Bloomfield

9-13-01

To my Baby:
enjoy this book!
It was written especially
for you!
I love you!
Love,
Gia xx

Anatomy Of A Sportfisherman

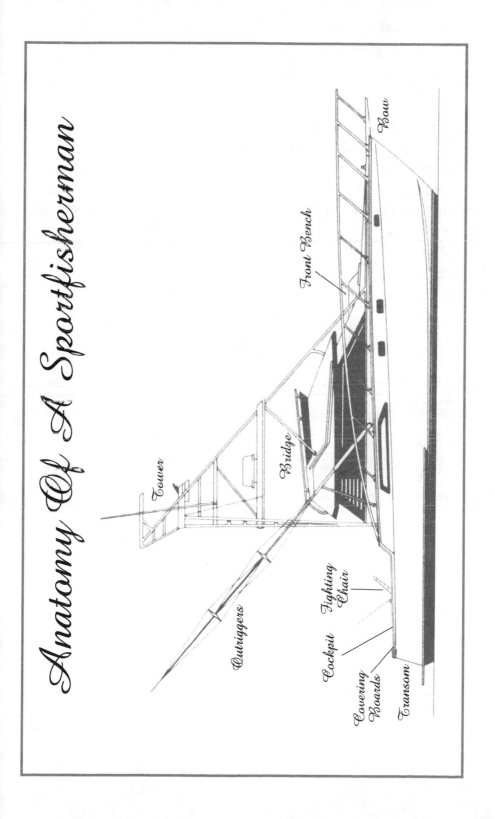

John Bloomfield

First Edition

ISBN: 0-9669007-0-7

Manufactured in the United States
R.R. Donnelley & Sons Company, Inc.
Jacket Design: Collins Doughtie Advertising, Hilton Head Island, South Carolina

Published and Distributed by;
        Fish On Company, Limited
        General Delivery
        Harbour Island, North Eleuthera
        Bahamas
        website: www.captainbo.com

This book is printed on acid free paper. The paper in this book meets the guidelines for permanence and durability of the Committee on Production Guidelines for Book Longevity of the Council on Library Resources.

This Book is Dedicated to my Wonderful Children,
Caroline and Wesley

Many thanks to my entire family,
my many friends, fishing buddies and friends
on Harbour Island, Bahamas,
for all your encouragement and support.

CHAPTER 1

Fish on! Right rigger!" screamed Bo. Zzzzzzzzzz! The 80-pound reel began screaming, louder than Bo, competing with him as the fish ran, dumping at least 500 yards of line a minute. Bulldog, all 400 pounds of him, rolled across the teak cockpit deck faster than a trimmer, younger mate ever could. Bo never saw any extremities, just the whole mass rolling.

Bulldog pounced on the rod and with one huge fist removed it from the rod holder and began pumping to set the hook, which was already set, but this was a game of reaction, not reason. The rod butt folded deep into his belly from the pressure. His other huge fist, looking more like a catcher's mitt than a human hand, soared high in the air, shaking defiantly at the fish and looking forward to the moment when it would unclench and extend into a triumphant high five.

The six paying guests stumbled all over themselves trying to remember Bo's simple instructions about what to do when they got a *fish on*. But some were drunk by then, and others were still drunk from the night before and never heard the instructions. The rest were incapacitated with seasickness, their faces literally ashen green which led the pros to call them "greenies." Actually, they were probably more help lying in their own puke than the drunk ones causing the confusion. Bo was used to it; it was his chosen profession.

From the bridge, while he frantically wound in teasers, he bellowed below, "You sons of bitches paid me twelve hundred bucks for this abuse, and now you're gonna get your money's worth!" Then, pointing, he ordered, "You, reel that rod in now! Yes, that one, you dumbass! You, get that one over there! Faster, dammit! Hurry!" Jesus, what a way to make a living, Bo bitched to himself.

"Bulldog, get somebody in the chair, so you can get the rest of the lines in." Bulldog turned, looking up at the bridge. His face looked just like his catcher's mitt hands, only bigger. "Who?" he shouted.

"Get one of the greenies," Bo yelled back. "It'll get his mind off it. He'll thank us later."

Bulldog reached down with his huge club hand and snatched the nearest one off the deck and tossed him into the chair. Poor guy never knew what happened. Bulldog was buckling the guy into the bucket harness, setting him up for the ride of his life, whether he wanted it or not.

Bo yelled, "Slick his ass!"

With one hand Bulldog yanked him up and with the other hand he squirted liquid soap on the twelve layers of varnish that protected and glorified the teak seat of the old Rybovich fighting chair. That chair was Bo's pride and joy. Once done, Bulldog plopped him back down and the poor sick guy nearly slid off the chair. Bulldog caught him and straightened him. It looked like a real bulldog playing with a rag doll. Bulldog finished getting the rod butt in the holder, and everything was set for the fight.

"Bull! This is a big fish," Bo yelled down. "Make sure he uses his legs, and keep him from trying to wind until I back down. Got it? And, Bull, get a safety line on that reel in case this marlin pulls him in the water. I guess you better put one on him too, if you've got time. If you don't, don't worry about it."

By now, the fish had quit her run and was taking a breather. The big billfish are females. She had dumped half a reel. The angler, the greenie, was starting to wake up as the other drunks popped fresh beers, took their positions, and cheered him on.

Bo yelled from the bridge, "She's goin' tight on us, she may dive, we're gonna back down on her." Very calmly and slowly, Bo continued, "As we back down, wind as fast as you can and don't let the line go slack." The only way to communicate with these guys was to treat them and talk to them as you would a small child - calmly and soothingly. Bo, facing aft, holding the transmission clutches in both hands, and with a perfect bird's-eye view of the action, hit reverse and revved. The backward motion of the boat caused the line to go slack.

"Wind, Motherfucker! Wind, wind, wind!" Bo shouted at the poor guy in the chair. The angler damn near jumped out of the chair, but Bulldog rested a paw on his shoulder. The sudden motion caused the angler to puke again and start blowing chunks of that morning's sausage everywhere, even into the thousand dollar gold reel. The drunks were whooping it up but not as loudly as Bo's bellowing. The angler did wind, as fast as he could, tears mixed with his vomit. The determination was admirable. This backing and winding continued for fifteen minutes, with the drunks hollering, and Bulldog hosing the angler down as stuff came up. Finally, the leader broke the surface, showing just ten yards of line before the hook and fish.

"It's critical now, gentle, gentle," Bo cautioned.

Seasoned Bulldog stood ready with the gaff, a pole with a razor-sharp hook on the end used to stick the fish and haul him onboard. Most mates wear two pair of gloves to wire a big fish. Bulldog never wore any; they were just naturally a part of his hands. Just as Bulldog reached for the leader, the sick angler, the greenie, had had enough and fell forward from exhaustion, hitting his head on the reel *and* the drag lever, freeing all the tension on the line and the fish.

The neon lighted-up billfish exploded out of the water, all 800-pounds of her, tail-walking completely out of the water. She shook her massive head back and forth so violently she threw that heavy plastic lure right back at the boat, hitting one of the drunks in the head and knocking his beer to the deck. Her defiance. She greyhounded, leaping and sailing to freedom.

Bo, pissed, just muttered, "Sonofabitch, sonofabitch." There was silence. The angler with the blood and vomit and tears looked as if he had mashed a box of strawberry-filled glazed donuts in his face. He just slouched back in the chair, half dead.

Bo announced, "Headin' for the hill."

As he steered the boat toward home, he revved the big diesels, and *Full Bloom* got on plane. Everyone took their places for the hour ride back. The angler was passed out in the chair. The drunks sought comfort by wedging themselves into various corners. Bulldog took his usual place, lying on the cockpit deck, but in the middle, as Bo made him do. His weight, other than centered, would affect the boat's performance. Bo looked down from the bridge at Bulldog, and smiled at his big buddy and hoped he wouldn't roll. With the autopilot on, Bo kicked back and said out loud to himself, "What a way to make a living."

The cruise back to the island was uneventful; everybody was asleep. Bo had run this route thousands of times but he never could, and he knew he never would, get over the beauty of that water. From his vantage point in the captain's chair on the bridge, he was 14 feet above the water. Bo could stare into it, and even through it. The color never ceased to amaze and calm him. Depending on the depth, the water turned from cobalt purple to brilliant neon green, then to azure turquoise. In fact, Bo always believed the color turquoise should have been named after that water, not the stone. The stone doesn't have that liquid magic depth. After years of looking for fish under the surface, his eyes naturally pierced deep into the gin clear water. He focused on infinity. He needed to; his present life was going nowhere.

Bo eased the 46-foot sportfisherman around and gently backed into his slip at the dock. He could dock that boat on a dime in his sleep. He knew that to be true because many times after a night of too much rum, he had awakened in the morning, stepped out into the blinding light of the bright sun reflecting off the white cockpit, and there she was, properly tied up, though Bo had no memory of doing it. A good boat is like a good dog, it always comes home. This one even puts itself to bed. To have a good dog you have to treat it right, and Bo treated his boat right. He had to; it was all he owned.

Some of the hotshot young captains, trying to appear macho, would hot-dog their owner's boats back into the slips to the point of leaving a wake. Bo recalled one young, loud idiot who plowed his owner's boat, *Sea Lion*, slap into the concrete dock, causing $100,000 worth of damage to the full teak transom. The transom, which looked like a piece of fine furniture, was turned into firewood in seconds, and the nice, *real* gold scripted name *Sea Lion* seemed to fall off in chunks. It's easy to be macho, on other people's money

CHAPTER 2

Tied up, plugged in and generator shut down, a couple of Bahamian schoolboys began the washing ritual while Bulldog tended to the rods, reels and tackle. Saltwater will, can, and does eat everything, like an acid. You have got to get it off, now. It *kills* machinery, but interestingly, is the closest natural composition on earth, to *life giving* blood. That's the Mother Ocean.

Bo usually fixed himself a rum and Coke and sat on the old rickety picnic table at the end of the dock, watching and thinking, sometimes about nothing, mostly about nothing. Today, watching and thinking only of the slender needle fish gliding by, a crossing shadow of a mast caught his attention.

"Fuck you!" echoed a voice in the harbor. "Lady, you and your slimy, snotty little kids aren't even bait, they ... they're not much better than chum. Correction, not even chum! You all can just eat shit. I ain't making one more *sammich* cause my ass is outta here," she yelled.

"You, and your perfect little family, can just fall off the edge of the flat sea in that stupid blow boat. Bitch!" she kept on.

The entertaining dialog was coming from a 42-foot sailboat sliding in with a gorgeous, blond, centerfold of a girl on the bow, feet planted and facing a nice-looking family unit with kids, all huddled in the boat's cockpit. *Miss Centerfold* was doing the talking, or yelling. The woman, the mother, was scrambling and gathering her young children to the protective custody of below decks, all the while trying to cover their tender ears.

The husband was trying to manage that confusion *and* dock the boat, without drawing any more attention. The trick to docking a boat is to do it as casually and effortlessly as possible. Hey, no big deal. A few skippers warrant the respect of not getting watched at all. Others, people hurry to help with the lines. The really bad skippers find the helpers hurrying away to avoid probable injury. This poor guy knew all respect was hopeless, and just continued. It couldn't be helped; he was committed now ... no turning back. As he tried to put the sailboat into the slip, *Miss Centerfold* jumped off and onto the dock as all eyes followed her. It was the best thing that could have happened to the skipper. He was no longer the center of attention.

She sashayed up to the bar. "Give me a Goombay Smash," she demanded of Sandy, the bartender. "Shit, give me the whole pitcher." Bo watched curiously, as he sipped his rum and grinned. New blood had found its way on the island, *hot* blood at that. Observers at the bar kept their distance and tried not to observe.

Bo threaded and glided his course through the maze of chairs that screened the bar. His walk, more so his entire presence, was like that of an effortlessly cruising Mako shark. You knew he wasn't going to strike; you may even look away, but you never, never really took your eyes off of him.

Bo sized up the situation, and figured, what the hell. "Enjoy your sail?" Bo asked.

"Eat shit, asshole," she shot back, even before she looked up and could take aim.

"Where'd you come in from?" Bo asked gentlemanly.

"Lauderdale." She turned her head back and swallowed half the first glass of smashes. Her neck was long and as liquid as the drink.

Bo again gently said, "I know it can be difficult on a boat with other people. It appears your trip was somewhat stressful." That was the most proper language he had ever used, and it surprised even him.

"Those little shits! Every time I wanted to lay out, they wanted some peanut butter and jelly sammiches, no fucking crust on the bread, little shits," she complained. "I hired on as a nanny, but there's no way I was gonna let those urchins keep me from my sun." She pulled her thong bottom sideways to let Bo see where the sun *did* shine. She was hot.

Bo kept quiet, letting her blow off steam and letting the ice in the smash cool her. Then he asked, "I've got some fresh tuna on my boat. You want some sushi?"

"NO! Go fuck yourself!" she spit as she stomped off up the breezeway.

"Sandy, put her pitcher on my tab," Bo said as got up to follow.

"Don't chase her, mon. She's a bad news boat bimbo," Sandy warned.

"Yeah, Sandy, I know, but I was born to fish and I'm draggin' baits now."

"I'll be still here, mon," said Sandy, rolling his eyes.

She was hurrying up the breezeway past the dive shop and into the street. Bahamians drive on the left side of the street, a hangover from being an English Crown Colony. She, being American, naturally looked left first, and then she stepped into the street. WHAM! A golf cart hit her doing all of five miles-per-hour, but that was enough for her to lose her balance, fall, and skin her knee.

"Man, these fuckin' dumb shits don't even know what goddamned side of the asshole street to run their baby piss-ant toys on. I can't get even a little shitty break," she screamed, grabbing her knee as blood began to ooze.

Bo rushed to her and asked, "You all right? You almost did get that break - a broken leg."

She started to cuss again, words Bo didn't even know. He helped her up, put her arm around his neck, "Come on, let's go get you fixed up."

They hobbled back toward the docks and Bo's boat, while she continued to mutter what Bo knew had to be a serious string of profanities.

As they passed, Sandy held out the rest of the pitcher of Goombay Smash, "You needs dis medicine for dat scrape, mon."

Bo settled her into the fighting chair. He didn't want to take her inside, no blood on the carpet. The cockpit had seen gallons of fish blood over the years, just hose it down. The fight was finally out of her, like a fish, and she just slumped back in the chair and drank the smash out of the pitcher.

Bo came out of the cabin carrying his first aid kit, "What's your name?"

"Darcy."

"Nice name, Darcy. I'm Bo, and this is my boat, *Full Bloom*. I charterfish for a living."

Bo sat on the chair's footrest, and she presented her wound. Darcy's legs were long and slender as a gazelle's and the same tawny color, too. She was a bona fide sun worshipper. With his hand, he gently cupped her calf and rested her leg on his thigh. Skin on skin. The feel of her leg and the thought of more teased his mind. Bo excitedly, but quietly, went about the cleaning and bandaging. So much for beauty being only skin deep, he thought; her blood was bright red, crimson red, challenging red. She sat and slurped from the pitcher. He looked up to check if she was all right and couldn't help grinning, he was seeing double, with only one rum in him. This was fun. He looked up again, and also worried he may just have run into double trouble too.

Bulldog came trundling down the dock, "What you catch there, Boss? Why did you gaff her?" He was serious.

Bo stood up and admired his medical handiwork.

"Gonna be fine, baby doll."

Then Bo noticed her flip-flops were on the wrong feet.

"I guess you were in such a rush to jump ship that you got your flip-flops on backwards." Darcy looked down.

"No they're not."

"They right, Boss," Bulldog agreed.

Hot Shit! Bo thought, I've just landed a gorgeous bimbo as dumb as Bulldog. He didn't want them smart; they were too much trouble when they could think. Fast water runs shallow. This girl was just as Bo liked them - fast and shallow.

CHAPTER 3

Bulldog had gone to Willie's Bar to play pool. Pool was the only activity Bulldog enjoyed, other than fishing. He was good, too. He actually made some money hustling the tourists, and nobody ever demanded their money back because of his size. He reminded folks of Jackie Gleason in the movies, *The Hustler*. Jackie had nothing on Bulldog, weight or otherwise.

The sun revealed only half of its disk, the other half being blocked by the horizon. With fresh rum and Cokes, and a squeeze of lime, Bo said, "Hey, Darcy, want to see something not many people have ever seen?"

"That sure wouldn't be your dick. Keep your pants on, big boy."

"No, no, no, come up here on the bridge. Watch your head on the way up," Bo said as he climbed the ladder to the bridge.

Thud. She hit her head climbing the ladder.

"Are you OK?"

"Sure."

Bo had hit his head on that cross piece before and it had brought tears to his eyes. Darcy acted as if nothing happened. Dumb *and* hardheaded! *Man!*

They sat on the bench seat in front of the control station.

"Keep your eyes right on the horizon near the sun," Bo said. "Exactly when the last little tip of the sun sinks below the horizon, we may see what is called the *green flash*. It's an event that's really not understood, but at that one moment a bright green glow will last about one second. We may not see it, because it only happens rarely under certain atmospheric conditions, but maybe we'll get lucky. I've seen it only twice in my life and I've watched for it thousands of times. It's a real phenomenon."

"What's a fucking phenomenon?"

"Just watch. Just watch. It could happen any second now," Bo said, staring and concentrating.

"Did you see it? Did you see it? Darcy! Did you see it?" Bo screamed, as he turned around toward her.

She was bent over, fiddling with her flip-flops.

"See what? These dumb things are hurting my feet."

CHAPTER 4

The night was one of those typical tropical spring nights in the Bahamas, warm, with a soft caressing breeze that every once in a while would just rustle the palms. Bo and Darcy were sipping on fresh rum and Cokes in the cockpit. Darcy was sitting in the fighting chair and Bo was sitting on the teak covering boards. Bo was proud of all the teak. To him it gave boats class and an older look that said "spare nothing and it ain't cheap." The newer boats didn't use all that teak because of maintenance and initial cost, but to Bo they looked so sterile with all that white fiberglass.

Darcy seemed to have mellowed out a little with the rum, so Bo went first.

"So how did you end up on that blow boat?" Bo asked.

"Well, I grew up in Lauderdale. I kinda went to high school there, but cut class every sunny day to 'lay out' on the beach. In my third year of the tenth grade, I quit."

"Quit laying out or quit school?"

"School, idiot. Home Ec was hard but study hall was okay, that's where I did my nails. They're shit now." She was studying them. "I did get an A in lunchroom once though."

"Lunchroom?"

"Yeah, I was a server, Bud, or whatever your name is. Peas or corn? Rice or potatoes? You know, tough choices to some of those dumb asses, so I helped them decide."

"Wow!" Bo said, trying to act impressed and amazed at her achievements but really he was just simply amazed.

"By then I was eighteen and could serve drinks instead of peas and corn, so I got a job waitressing. It was great because I could lay out all day, make money at night and sleep 'til noon. My mom always said I could do better but she was the only one who ever believed in me.

"I was going on my fourth year in my career when this guy comes in the bar and we start chatting; it's my job, you know. He asked me to wait around and talk to him after closing. He said he had a 'proposition'. I said, 'Sure, old man, fuck you and the horse you rode in on. I'm a lesbian.' "

"You *are?* Really? Are you?" Bo asked disappointedly.

She laughed mysteriously. Bo thought, well so much for this adventure. Then he thought, maybe she's just teasing. He hoped.

"Anyway, he said he and his wife had two kids. He said they had a 42-foot sailboat and wanted to sail the Bahamas. They were looking for some single girl to go with them to take care of the kids so they could enjoy the cruise together. I had other friends do it and they had fun. I had never seen the Bahamas so I said, yes. After all, I am a professional server, peas and corn, whiskey and beer, and now Pop-Tarts and Twinkies. What the shit, it don't matter. He said they were leaving in a week. I turned in my notice and the key to my room and jumped on.

"Right from the start his wife didn't like me worth a damn. All I did was ask her where do I throw my shit, and she got real tight-lipped. I mean, her lips were tighter than an asshole on the edge of a thousand-foot cliff. Anyway, she said, 'My dear, you may stow your gear in the mid-ship starboard locker.' I said, I ain't got gears in here lady. This is my bag of shit. She walked down the dock and started yelling at the old man. I sat on the dock and filed my nails. In a little while the old man came back and said that even though we didn't hit it off, he convinced her to at least give it the old college try for the first leg of the trip. I told him I didn't know nothin' about college and asked him what the hell he was talking about.

He said I could go, and he stowed my bag of shit for me. By the way, I never did find it. That's why I ain't got it with me now."

Darcy pulled at the straining top string of the tiny thong suit. It seemed all out of proportion to the task.

"Same suit I had on when I left. We pulled out and went under the 17th Street drawbridge. That was cool. In all the years I have waited at that bridge for some piss-ant boat to go under and get out of my fucking way; it was neat for me to be stopping traffic now."

"Stop right there," Bo said. "Let me freshen these. I don't want to miss a second of your fantastic life's journey."

She handed him her glass and smiled, a smile with perfectly, straight, white teeth. God sure put all his effort into the looks of this one, but He must have gotten plain worn out and quit when it came to filling her pretty head, Bo thought. He returned with the drinks.

"You're not a bad server yourself, buddy," she said.

"I didn't get an A, though," he replied.

"Oh, that's okay," she said, seriously sympathetic.

"I had just got my towel straight on the front deck to lay out and this little munchkin pops his head up out of this hatch right next to me and says, 'I want a peanut butter and jelly sammich.' I said, 'Excuse me, little fart, you talking to me?' He ducks in and I hear him screaming, 'Mommy, Mommy, she said a bad word.' The old man comes up on the deck and says, 'Now Darcy, that is your job. You need to take care of the little ones while mommy takes her nap.' Jeeze. So I go down below and find the shit and fix both the little squirts a sammich. That's what they call it, 'sammich.' I know better; it's sandwich. I gave him a napkin and everything. I'm real proud. Then this little turd starts crying and tells me he can't eat the fucking crust and to cut it off. Now I'm a professional server, but, Christ! Well, I did it for him anyhow. Ain't I something?"

"Yes, Darcy, you really are," Bo said. "You really are."

"It went on like that since yesterday morning when we left Lauderdale: do this, do that, get this, get that. I didn't get but maybe six hours of layin' out in. By the time I got here, I had had it with the whole fucking mess. I jumped ship as soon as I could reach a dock."

"I know. I heard you," Bo said. "The whole dock heard you."

"You know you're not a bad looking guy, Bud, Bo, whoever you are."

"Bo. Too much rum, Darcy," Bo said modestly.

Bo had a lean hard body from outdoor work on the high seas and a tan almost as dark as Darcy's. However, Bo got his tan as a consequence of his job, not from vanity. He had just turned thirty and was only about 5' 10" and 165 pounds, but you could tell the strength was there. The most striking feature were his eyes. They were the color of the water he plowed his boat through. They were damn near turquoise and so bright they looked as if light was originating from inside instead of reflecting off of them. Maybe after all those years of looking into that water, his eyes had simply absorbed it, like osmosis.

"What about you?" Darcy asked. "How'd you get here?"

"That's a long story," Bo said with a sigh.

"Well, I just told you my whole life story."

"That was your *whole* life story?" Bo said incredulously.

"Yeah, that's pretty much it. How did you get this boat? How could somebody as young as you afford this boat? How did you learn to fish? Shit like that." Darcy really seemed interested.

"I didn't get past the tenth grade either, but I quit on my first try. I was too into flying airplanes. I worked as a line boy at the local airport pumping gas and stuff in trade for flying lessons. I lied to the FAA about my age and got my license at fourteen. It was funny; my Dad had to give me a ride to the airport because I had no driver's license for a car, just to fly a plane. Then this guy flies in on a P-51. That's a World War II fighter plane. I damn near creamed in my jeans. It was the most beautiful machine I had ever seen. I just wanted to touch it, and just as I was about to, the guy comes around the corner of the hanger and yells, 'Touch it and I'll lock you in the bomb bay and use you as a human bomb from 10,000 feet.' Then he just laughed and said he was kidding. He appreciated my appreciation. We struck up a conversation and I told him I was a pretty good pilot. Actually, I bragged.

"He asked me if I wanted a job flying and I almost died right there. My life's dream. This guy said he owned a crop dusting operation and worked out of middle Georgia and, oh, by the way, his name was Deet, for DDT, that's a pesticide. I went to work flying a big yellow Ag-Cat."

"I had a cat once. I killed it when one of the concrete blocks holding up my bed broke. He was under it."

"What were you doing? Forget it. Ag means agriculture. That's a duster/sprayer airplane. God, it was fun! Crop flying was like stunt flying - low flying, tight turns, steep dives, full power climbs and landing on the highway. I did that for three years with Deet. There were four of us, and we traveled all around the Southeast. The only bad part was having to handle and breathe that shit all day. It stunk."

"The lunchroom didn't smell too good either," Darcy added.

"Right." Bo was in his own reminiscent world.

"In our minds we were as tough as test pilots and probably more cocky. Then, when I was eighteen, I met this dude in a bar, just like you did with that guy. I told him what I did; I always told everybody. I was proud, and flying was my identity. He specifically asked about family, like, if I had one, if they knew where I was and stuff, real personal. I told him I had just run off to fly and nobody really cared. Perfect, he said. He handed me his card as he left, and told me to call him when I really wanted to make money. The card said Mr. J.T. Thorn, Special Agent, AirAmerica. Well, I called. You won't believe the job he was selling. He wanted me to fly small planes in Laos."

"I got louse in my hair once. It was in kindergarten. My momma washed me with dog soap. I kinda liked it."

"Anyway, he said AirAmerica had contracts with the CIA to fly spooks and spies around. They would pay me $2,000 per week."

"Shit, man, I could only dream about that kind of money," Darcy whispered.

"It was unbelievable. I never made that much in a whole season crop dusting. The catch was I could not tell one soul were I was or what I was doing. I told him that's no big catch. Also, he said I could get shot at, and if I got shot down, nobody would come and everybody would say they did not even know my name. I would be left on my own. No problem again. I was on my own anyway, and what the hell? I was ten-foot tall and bulletproof. I signed on. I could fly. Well, I got shot at plenty, but never got hit. The plane did, though. We were always coming back with holes in the planes. One time, I really got sprayed. The next morning we counted 48 bullet holes. And you won't believe this, but my boss was pissed 'cause the plane was down for two weeks. And to make it worse, he made *me* help fix it.

"Some guys didn't come back at all. That's the part I don't talk about. I guess I just don't want to remember it ... but I do. A lot of it was boring, though; it wasn't all excitement. We'd sit around all day playing cards and shit and fly mostly at night. There was a river nearby, and even then I loved to fish. I was going to save my money and not lose it playing poker, so I started fishing instead to take up my time and get away from the cards. I couldn't find any hooks and line, but supply had screwed up and sent over ten cases of these sewing kits."

"Sewing, that's why I fucking flunked Home Ec," Darcy contributed.

"Right. With so much thread and safety pins, I had enough tackle to last the whole damn war. About a couple of months before I left, I quit fishing. One day I was daydreaming of this boat we're on right now, when four grotesque, bloated bodies floated by, just grinning like dead pigs in the August sun. I dropped my cane pole right there and walked back, all the while thinking about all the fish I had eaten out of that river."

"Peas or corn. Rice or potatoes," said Darcy.

"We had no expenses so I could save every penny to buy a battlewagon sportfisherman and fish for a living, forever. I did it for a year and left that God-forsaken dump with over a $100,000 in my pocket. When I got back to the States, I went to Deet and convinced him to co-sign a bank note for another $100,000 and I bought the *Full Bloom* you're sitting on right here."

"Jeeze, I had no friggin' idea this boat cost that much!" Darcy exclaimed. "You're rich. I'm starting to like you more now."

"Shit, I barely pay the bills. You add up dockage, fuel, Bulldog, bait, insurance, maintenance, not to mention the monthly bank note, I ain't got squat. I want a bigger boat so I can take more people out and really make some bucks, but there's no way I can see that happening."

"I want to make some big bucks, too. I want a shiny red BMW convertible, a nice condo in Palm Beach and some new nails, shiny red, too, all of them. Plus, even though I am a professional server, you know, I don't want to *have* to work so I could just lay out all day and party all fuckin' night. But just like you, buddy Bo, I can't see that shit happenin' either," Darcy said with a deep sigh.

"This island could support a bigger boat. I had a friend vacation here who wanted to charter a boat to fish for a day, but nobody had anything more than little bay boats. That's why I decided to come here. Virgin territory," Bo reasoned.

"Virgin territory, what's that? I don't believe there is a virgin anything anymore," Darcy exclaimed.

"*You* wouldn't know. Are you really a lesbo?" Bo teased.

She laughed that laugh again.

"Money, money, money, money!" She sang the song and reality brought Bo around.

"If I could just *find* some money. I need cash, dammit! If I could just find some money," Bo said, wishing on the star. He lay back on the covering boards with his hands folded behind his head and wished upon every star he saw until he got tired of the monotony and simply put in for a blanket wish from all of them.

He sat up. Darcy was asleep, her chest was holding up her chin. He gently lifted her out of the fighting chair and carried her inside the cabin to the sofa. As he laid her down, one of her huge, delicious breasts fell out of its sling. He wanted to feel it, just touch it, like the P-51, but caught himself; not going to get it by stealing. He was going to get it fair and square, by God.

Bo got a blanket and gently covered her. As he turned to head to his stateroom, he stopped. He carefully removed her flip-flops and placed them side by side, the *right* way. It was going to be interesting to see which feet they were on in the morning.

CHAPTER 5

When Bo opened his eyes the next morning, he could see through the hatch above him. It was starting out to be a bright and sunny day. He didn't have a trip that day, so he had planned on catching up on several chores. He slid his six-pocket fishing shorts on and a T-shirt that proclaimed biblically, "I Fish Therefore I Am." Am *what*?, he thought. He guessed whatever he wanted to be at the moment, but having that responsibility seemed like a burden right now.

That worried him. He was the captain of his own life. Captain of a boat, hell, that was okay. He could handle that, but captain of *his* life was too much. He'd rather just be the mate.

In the galley he threw a cup of water in the microwave for coffee. Then he remembered Darcy and grabbed another for her. He didn't know if she drank coffee or not, but he would be a gracious host. Darcy was asleep on the sofa, as he had left her. She looked so peaceful asleep. What does she turn into when she wakes up? Bo thought about Bulldog, and now her, and how happy and peaceful they both seemed. Dumb is better. The aroma of the coffee woke her up.

"Mornin'!" he said cheerfully.

"Eat shit! What kind of rum was that anyway?"

"Mount Gay," he replied

"Mount a gay, what a faggot name. No wonder I feel like shit."

"I thought you'd like it," he said. Maybe, just maybe, there is hope.

"I'm starving, but I've got to take a friggin' shower first," she said, rustling her hair and checking her body like, where have you been?

"It's right here," he said and showed her the way to the head.

"I need a toothbrush, too. I'll just use yours." Bo was a little funny about stuff like that, but then he remembered her perfect teeth and thought what the hell.

As she was showering, Bo went outside on the dock to check his live baits. The fish were captured and corralled in a mesh trap floating in the water and tied to the dock. Barracuda were always lurking under the dock's pilings, eyeing the easy dinner, and no matter what Bo did to scare them off, they just wouldn't learn. Maybe they had their fins on backwards. All was well with the baits, so Bo decided to chamois the morning dew off the boat himself, since he had given Bulldog the day off.

Darcy came out, hair still wet but woven into a French braid and no make up; she didn't need it. Bo thought, all she needs is a bathing suit, a toothbrush, and flip-flops marked R and L with an indelible laundry marker. At that thought he looked down, and damn if it wasn't so - they were on the wrong feet again. He was beginning to question *himself*.

"Come on, I know where we can get the best breakfast on the island," he announced.

They strolled off the dock, past the bar, through the breezeway and into the street. Harbor Island is called Briland by the local Bahamians. Bo guessed they figured, why go to all the effort with all those syllables, just shorten it up. Make it easy, no problem, mon, the Bahamian way.

The center of Briland is Dunmore Town or, again making it easy, just Dunmore. Dunmore was a Lord from England, and the town was declared the first capital of the Bahamas. The King of England had granted the Loyalists the land in the 1700s as their reward for remaining faithful to the Crown while the

Revolutionaries in the Colonies rebelled. Most were wealthy plantation owners who had come from South Carolina, North Carolina and Georgia. Some had big plans of re-creating their massive plantations down in the Bahamas. Many even went so far as to tear down their old plantation homes, brick by brick, and used those bricks as ship's ballast so they could rebuild in Dunmore. Unfortunately, on the sea voyage, the bilge water on board turned the bricks into mush.

Without the bricks and with only a limited wood supply available on the islands, they resorted to building smaller cottages. The initially noticeable and curious feature of these cottages was their size; not their total physical size but the size of the doors and windows which were much smaller than what most homes have today since the people were of smaller stature back then. George Washington, standing at six feet, was considered to be a big man. The architecture looks like that of the old, restored towns, such as Williamsburg, in the States. The one difference is the colors. All the cottages are painted in the Bahama colors of pink, light blue, white, and yellow.

The soil in the Bahamas wouldn't support the kind of agriculture they had back home. Since the plantation system failed in the Bahamas, subsequent generations of the wealthy elite owners were reduced to the level of squatters and the slaves they had brought with them were left to fend for themselves. The overwhelming black population of the Bahamas is the ancestry of those slaves.

Bo and Darcy were headed up the street toward Ma Ruby's for breakfast. Ma Ruby's place was located on the Queen's Highway, which is only a one and a half lane, pot-holed road. Every island in the Bahamas has a Queen's Highway, no matter how small the island. All that is necessary to qualify and be sanctioned the Queen's Highway is for it to be the main drag, whether it be a paved road, a dirt road, or only a macheteed foot path. Being the main drag, even if it's the only drag, is the ticket to the designation.

Ma Ruby was probably 70 years old, though no one really knew or cared. She had the friendliest face and attitude Bo had ever known. Bo kept a relaxed, running tab with her restaurant, trading fresh fish for meals. Ma Ruby's restaurant was an open-air affair but with a permanent roof structure. A couple of the white lattice walls opened to the small bar and restrooms. Palms swayed all around, and bougainvillea blossomed everywhere. It was clean as the tropical breeze and bright with the sun. Ma Ruby's daughter, Juanita, had a cheerful face as well. The restaurant was just the place to cleanse a drinking night's fog from the head. Bo breakfasted here almost every morning.

"You won't believe the French toast here, as fine as your French braid," Bo told Darcy as he admired the natural blond color of her hair.

"Good mornin', Bo!" Ma Ruby and Juanita chorused in unison.

"Hi, Ma Ruby. Hi, Juanita. How are y'all this morning?" Bo responded.

"Just fine, Bo, just fine," everyone replied.

"Ma Ruby, this is Darcy. She was crewing on a sailboat but decided it wasn't to her liking. I'm helping her find other work. You wouldn't happen to have any ideas would you?" Bo asked.

"Ma Ruby, I'm a professional server. Maybe I could work here. Do you serve peas or corn and rice or potatoes?" Darcy lit up.

"Dear, we do serve peas and rice," Ma Ruby said.

"Together? No choices? I'm not sure, Bo," Darcy seemed disappointed.

"My family, all my three children work for me. I don't need any help now, but I'll keep you in mind, sweetie," Ma Ruby said.

"Juanita, French toast, bacon, juice, and coffee for two," Bo announced. Bahamian French toast is the best and it's even better at Ma Ruby's. Bo figured it was the bread; Bahamian bread is almost like cake to start with.

Juanita went about setting the table and placing the order, but before she went to the kitchen, she went to the grounds and picked a handful of fresh bougainvillea to place as a centerpiece on the table. The food came quickly, unusual for the Bahamas, but they were always ready for Bo. Darcy ate like a shark. She was sopping up the last little bit of syrup while Bo still had two pieces left on his plate. Bo was again amazed and thought this girl must have a tapeworm or something, to eat like that and have such a body.

Bo finished and they bid Ma Ruby a farewell. They headed back out into the brilliant sun and walked back down the Queen's Highway. A couple of blocks later they were at Uncle Ulmer's "Prophecy Corner." Uncle Ulmer was one of Bo's best friends and his personal mentor. Ulmer was kicked back in a lawn chair missing half the straps, his butt hanging through like a reverse pregnancy. Even though it was 10 o'clock in the morning, Ulmer was drinking a real dark beer out of a plastic cup. He never drank out of the bottle; he just couldn't get enough, as fast as he wanted, when he wanted. Little things like big gulps are important.

"What's today's proverb, Ulmer?" Bo asked, startling him from his stupor or deep thoughts. Bo couldn't tell and Ulmer didn't know. Ulmer painted proverbs and other notable bits of wisdom on wood. Driftwood, plywood, whatever he could find. He sold them to tourists who prized them and mounted them in prestigious places in their expensive homes. There were hundreds displayed and hanging in the trees at Uncle Ulmer's "Prophecy Corner."

"Hey, Bo, and Dahling!" Ulmer exclaimed. "Wait right here, Dahling, right here, I be right back," said Ulmer, as he was running around the corner to his house. In thirty seconds Ulmer came stumbling back, totally concentrating. All the concentration powers he had were focused on his right hand. He was tenderly carrying his treasure as someone would carry an injured baby bird. When he got to Darcy, he slowly unfolded his hand and revealed a flower.

"It's a passion flower, Dahling, just for your beautifulness," Ulmer said as he was placing the flower in her hair, behind her ear.

Bo had seen this ritual hundreds of times. When Bo witnessed Ulmer's flower tithing in the beginning of their friendship, he thought, where does he get all these exotic flowers? He never runs out. Bo ate one once to test if it was plastic or real. It was real.

Uncle Ulmer always dressed and looked the same way. He always sported a bandanna around his head and wore torn, stretched out T-shirts with arm holes down to his waist, and old sandals. Paint was splattered on his complete attire and skin from sign work or house painting, which he did on occasion. However, painting proverbs was his day job, and the house painting was not even the night job, just sometimes. One other enjoyable constancy was his pleasant smile and energetic, overly enthusiastic style. Bo always thought Ulmer was what the Bahamas were really all about. Ulmer never had any money and never had any worries. He was the happiest man Bo had ever met. Bo always worried about money. One day, Bo told himself, I've got to get Ulmer to share his secret.

"Well, Ulmer, I've got to get back to the boat and do some chores," Bo said.

"Thanks for the flower, Mr., uh, Uncle Ulmer."

"Always my pleasure, Dahling, see you later." Ulmer headed across the street for another beer.

"I need to lay out, just look at this sun," Darcy said.

"Sure. Do you know how to snorkel?" Bo asked.

"I've done it a couple of times. It's pretty easy."

"While I work, why don't we get you some gear? You can go to the beach, lay out, and snorkel. Some of the world's most beautiful reefs are right off the beach, only 50 yards out."

On the way back to the boat, they stopped in the dive shop and fitted Darcy with some gear and Hot-Bod tanning oil, SPF *minus* 15 or something. Bo gave her directions to the beach, which were no more than go straight, do not turn, and stop when you get wet. He gave her a little running start as an adult does when, for the first time, the kid's training wheels are taken off the bike. He hoped she could make it. Another comforting thought was the fact that flippers are uni-feet, no left or right.

CHAPTER 6

As Bo was walking down the breezeway to the dock, Cora Lee, Valentine Marina's bookkeeper, called out, "Bo, you've got a telly call." Bo picked up his pace for the office.

"Hello, you got Bo. Tight lines to ya," was Bo's stock greeting and finishing fishing signature. It meant you had a big 'fish on' and the fish was pulling hard.

"Bo, this is Atom," the other end echoed with a half second delay because it was an international call. That annoying delay always made conversation staccato and not really conversation at all, but a string of short burst messages. Atom was a Ph.D. in physics at Georgia Tech and internationally renowned. He had the most brilliant mind Bo had ever known. Atom's given birth name was Adam but was changed legally to Atom somewhere along the pathway of eons and light-years of physics schooling.

"Hey, man. How you been? Where are you? What's up?"

"Bo, I've got to come to Nassau to chair a lecture in two days."

"Great, do you have time to come over to the island?"

"Actually, I could come early this afternoon. Think we could fish tomorrow?"

"No charter tomorrow. Sure, man," Bo replied.

"See you at the dock at 1600 hours this afternoon. Get the blender warmed up for some cool ones." Click.

Bo thanked Cora Lee and sauntered back to the boat.

A year ago *Full Bloom's* starboard engine had begun smoking. It had gotten progressively worse, and each time Bo saw it, he told himself he'd better check it out. But he didn't. He was afraid of what he might find, to the point of every time he cranked the big diesel, he would look forward away from the exhaust so he didn't have to see it. Out of sight, out of mind ... but not really. It weighed heavily on him. Last week he made an appointment with himself to check it out. Today was the day. It was almost like having to set a dreaded date to stop smoking. He wished it were that easy.

Bo changed into shorts that already had grease and oil stains covering them. He couldn't get in the engine room for five seconds without some oil just jumping right out of some fitting and onto him. Armed with a flashlight and a wrench, Bo crawled and wiggled and snaked his body to the outboard side of the big diesel. Lying down and propped up on one elbow, he used the wrench to pop open the inspection plates. With the flashlight he could peer all the way into the massive cylinders. His worst nightmare was confirmed. Two cylinder wall sleeves were cracked. That meant re-sleeving the entire engine. Big diesels are $40,000 each, and a major job like the one he was staring at would run $5,000. He just lay there not thinking, numb, while oil dripped on his head.

Bo washed up and changed his clothes. He warmed up the blender ahead of schedule and while he was sipping his first smash, he threw in a cassette. The speakers wailed, "I'm getting *real good* at just gettin by." No shit, not even that, not even good, much less *real good*, Bo thought. Five grand minimum, damn, Bo kept thinking and worrying. That meant a mechanic from the States. He would have to be smuggled in since Bahamian Immigration allowed "no meaningful work" from her guests. That means the whole Bahamian population must be guests. Plus, that mechanic would cost time and a half for being out of the country, lodging, food and probably entertainment.

Entertainment would be easy, though, cheap rum and midnight basketball at the Vikum, Ma Ruby's son's nightclub. Bo knew first-hand, although it took dozens of tries, that midnight basketball was

no way to solve the inner city adolescent social and crime problems. All his studies, which he diligently and personally performed,
had proven to end up in disaster. At any rate, there was no question
he would have been safer and more sober staying in his own bunk
at a reasonable hour. A ten-foot basket gets tall from your knees,
and right now he was feeling just as low. Bo just had to face it, he
had to find some money; he just *had* to find some money. But
where? Where?

Fixing his second drink, Bo remembered Atom would be there
in a couple of hours. Atom wanted to fish and he needed baits.
Bulldog rigged all the ballyhoo baits and normal bottom fishing
stuff and was pretty good at it. But those really special blue marlin
baits were magic and only Bonefish Joe could catch those baits and
rig them properly.

Just like the Queen's Highway, every island had a Bonefish Joe.
Unlike the singular Queen's Highway, some islands had several
Bonefish Joe's. Bo always thought it would be interesting to take
some of them back in time to the old TV show "To Tell The Truth."
On the show the contestants had to choose the real person over
some impostors by virtue of the answers they provided. Several
Bonefish Joes could shut the whole thing down. All the Bonefish
Joes Bo had ever met never lied. They didn't know the truth,
which, given enough time, is true of all fishermen.

On Channel 16, the hailing channel on the radio, Bo barked,
"Bonefish Joe, Bonefish Joe, come back to the *Full Bloom*." A few
seconds went by.

"*Full Bloom, Full Bloom*, how you feelin', Bo? Go to one-two,
one-two," Bonefish responded. One-two meant channel 12, which
is dedicated for conversations.

"One-two," Bo acknowledged, and switched his radio.

"Joe, how ya doin?" Bo connected.

"Mighty fine, Bo, mighty fine."

"I need a dozen sparklers for tomorrow. I don't know how early we're gonna leave, so you better bring them this afternoon. You got any?"

"For you, Bo, always. I be right dare."

Bahamian time might as well be another time zone. "No problem, mon, tomorrow" always means next week at best, next month if you're lucky and sometimes, many times, never. The few things that don't operate on that time scale, but actually operate on hyperspeed, is the delivery of golf carts, baits, and whiskey. These goods are brought right to your door in minutes. Bo hadn't tried women yet, but he had heard.

Sure as shark shit, Joe was by in a couple of minutes.

"Hey Bo, get dat country tune offen, en puts on some island tunes; you gets mo fish, mon." He held up a dozen sparklers, all rigged fresh.

The wire leaders were coiled perfectly, the proper weights were snug beneath the lower lip, and new hooks that had entered the fish under its gills protruded out and curled forward from their anuses straight, sharp, and ready. The fish that was the prized bait was, naturally, the bonefish. This fish was the perfect size for big blue marlin baits, about one to two pounds. They were special because marlin are attracted to flashing light, and these bonefish had thousands of scales and each one looked like a miniature CD caught and twisted in sunlight. As they were pulled through the water, the sun would reflect off their scales and the whole rainbow would sparkle off each scale differently.

"As always, Joe, great lookin' baits," Bo said as he went into the cabin to get money. Joe didn't take anybody's credit. He lived by that creed, "In God we trust, all fishermen pay cash, except for Peter, but he was a fisher of men," or something like that.

"Hey, Bo," Joe caught him before he had gotten in the cabin.
"Yeah?"

"I's to up a lil on de prices, granchiles en all, you can figgur."
Bo waited.

"I's got to get five dollar de bait at de present," Joe said bashfully. Last week's price was four.

"Damn Joe, I'm going to have to start catching my own," Bo declared, knowing he never would. Joe knew that, too. It was just old time haggling begun thousands of years ago.

"I's da best en dese magic baits does catch da big momma marlin, mon."

"All right, this time, Joe," Bo said. Joe cheered up, glad his buddy Bo wasn't giving him a harder time.

"Hey Bo! You knows I's da *Masterbaiter*."

"Beat it, Joe." Bo handed him the money.

———◆———

Bo gently placed the baits in the refrigerator, laying them side by side and alternating tail to head, so the bodies would nest and they would lie flat. The rest of the refrigerator was an absolute infectious waste mess, but there was something about laying those baits in perfectly that Bo instinctually did. Priorities.

Back up on the bridge, Bo kicked back with the next frozen mixture in a full double walled 16-ounce cup to ponder his problem. As he was thinking, or trying not to think, a big 50-foot brand new Post Sportfish was backing in across the dock from him. Crisp uniforms were on the captain and crew, and as they handled the boat and the lines, Bo could tell they knew the drill. Everything was matched and color coordinated. The blue shorts the crew wore matched the dock lines, which matched the accent stripes, which matched the chair cover and on and on. Bo laughed to himself that the blue showing on their color depth finder background was a slightly different shade of blue than the rest. He bet they tried, though.

In truth, Bo was green with envy, and making fun of the eccentric detail was his way of telling himself he was not. He wanted a bigger boat and one like that. If it were his, he bet Atom could change that screen color, and Bo would have him do it, too. Thinking of *that* made the reality hit him even harder, daydreaming of color on the screen, while his own boat was looking at a $5,000 overhaul just to run. I've got to find some money, Bo thought. I've just got to find some money. Where? Where?

"Bo! Hey, Bo!" Atom yelled as he walked down the dock. Bo looked at his watch. Where had the day gone?

"Hey, mon, good to see you," Bo smiled as he yelled back. Bo was looking at a green checkered shirt, purple striped pants, an orange florescent cap, and, to complete the ensemble, black knee socks under Roman warrior-looking sandals. Atom was the complete opposite of the Post that had just pulled in. Bo wanted to tell him he had just bought that Post, and to jump on board, just to give the owner a heart attack. It wasn't that Atom didn't give a shit. You have to be conscious to give a shit or not. Atom just had no idea. That was one of the many things Bo liked about Atom.

As he got closer, Bo could see the latest, turbo-pumped mini-computer hanging off his belt, all in the ready for a quick draw should some pesky physics problem attack him. Also, Bo noticed, and then he remembered the big black, indelible pen Atom carried in his shirt pocket. Atom was always right, and to prove it, he always wrote in indelible ink, no erasing, no going back. Bo thought of Darcy's flip-flops; he could use that pen.

"Let me help you with your grip," Bo said, standing in the cockpit. He grabbed an avocado green, hardback Samsonite with one busted latch that duct tape had replaced, circa 1958. Atom's mother had handed it down to him on his way to Georgia Tech.

"Boat's looking great," Atom said, surveying the teak.

"Yeah, well, I've got some problems. Come on, let's get you a Goombay Smash. Go up on the bridge. I'll get it for you. Watch your head."

Bo returned with a big cup for Atom and his own cup replenished. "So, why are you in Nassau?" he asked.

"I am chairing a council on quantum quarks getting lost in black holes. Naturally, they always hold these things where there is sun and sand, so the spouses don't mind coming. I'd rather go to some-place more exotic, like the North Pole." Exotic to Atom was some-where he could study, witness, and then figure out some inexplica-ble natural phenomenon.

"Well, its good to see you. Who dressed you?"

"How is the fishing?" The dressing question went right over his head.

"Been pretty good. Last week we pulled in six wahoo, one was 78 pounds; nine dolphin, a bull at 60 pounds; eight tuna, and yes-terday lost a big blue right at the boat. The bite's been good."

"How did you lose the blue?" inquired Atom who lived by eat-ing, drinking and digesting physics mysteries, and fishing was his only diversion. He knew the sport, and had become fairly good at it, thanks to Bo's tutelage.

"That's a story for later. I have to have some more of these smashes to be in the same condition as the angler who lost her, so I can give it justice ... and sympathy."

"How is Bulldog?"

"Bulldog is Bulldog and that, as you know, is fine; he's a rock - a damn boulder. He's already working on his Santa outfit and has stowed away $500. He's got a heart of gold. Paying for toys from the pool hustling money. He just loves those kids, and they love him back. You know a lot of kids on this island wouldn't have Christmas if it weren't for Bull. You know, even those kids who do get toys from their parents believe he's the real Santa, and they get the stuff from him. Oh yeah, I met this gorgeous girl, dumber than a conch."

"Say not! None of your lady friends are too bright, however," Atom said.

"Yeah!"

"I mean so dumb she wears her flip-flops on the wrong feet, and can't understand why her feet hurt. She's a real boat bimbo, but I think she's kind of a gold digger too. She thinks I have money because of the boat. I'll just play with her for a while, until she jumps ship to the next guy's boat. They always do. Or, I'll get tired of her and run her off when I'm finished. I don't know what will come of it."

"Have you partaken of the flesh yet?"

"What? No. I just met her yesterday, but it probably won't be long. She's so stupid, though, she might just ask me what I'm doin'. Maybe not, she talks like she knows what she's doin'. Oh! She says she's a lesbo, but I don't believe it. I'm gonna find out, though."

"What's a lesbo?"

"A lezzi. A *lesbian*, Atom."

"Where is she?"

"I sent her to the beach, but we'll have to go collect her I reckon. No way she can find her own way back, if she even got there."

"*Full Bloom, Full Bloom* ... Michael Cycle." The VHF radio announced on channel 16.

Bo got up and grabbed the microphone, "Michael, go to one-four, one-four," Bo said as he changed channels.

"Bo, I got dis girl here dat sez she be on you boat. Sez she be lost an belong to you. Want me bring she roun'?"

"Yeah, Michael, I appreciate it. *Full Bloom* back to 16."

Atom laughed, "*Belong to you*. Sounds like a lost puppy."

"Wait tell you see those pups," Bo said.

"I got to go to the head," Atom said, as he was getting up to go below.

"I better make another pitcher full. That girl can *drink*. Oh, use mine, the guest head is down. Somebody threw another damn tampon in it. I swear I ought to call Tampax and buy a roll of that string stuff for leader line," Bo said as he followed him inside. This happened at least a couple of times a year despite the big plaque posted above the head that ordered, "Do Not Throw Anything In The Head Unless You Have Eaten It First."

Bo was back in the fighting chair, and Atom was sitting on the covering boards looking up the dock. "Thermo-dynamic," Atom softly said.

"What?" Bo said. "Darcy! This my friend Atom."

"Hey, cool outfit."

"You get lost?" Bo asked, already knowing. He just wanted to hear the story.

"Shit, yeah. I got to the beach fine, but on the friggin' way back I came to this corner and didn't remember which way. I went right or left, I don't remember. But I'm used to square blocks, so I kept going, like around, in the same direction, counting the corners, tryin' to get to four, but damn if I couldn't count but three, and I'd be back to where I fuckin' started."

"Can you count to four?" Bo said with a laugh. He knew where she had been. The town had a triangular block up by the hardware store.

"Fuck you, buddy Bo."

"I'm just teasing."

"Just curious, but why did you do that anyway?" Atom asked. "What had you hoped to accomplish?"

"I don't know. I figured, I'd end up some damn where."

"But even if the block had *four* corners as you are accustomed, you would still be going in circles," Atom said.

Bo thought, maybe she's, or he's, kind of right. Most of the corners he thought he had turned in his life lately had led right back to the beginning. Just going in circles.

"Don't worry your pretty little head about it." Bo's patronizing comment was only a macho cover up meant for Atom's consumption. He couldn't believe Darcy let him get away with it.

"Have a smash. You're home now," Bo said. Did I say *home*? Shit, Bo.

"Bo, Darcy, I've been traveling all day," Atom said. "If you don't mind, I'm going to take a nap, so I can be mobile tonight."

"You got a mobile home?" Darcy asked.

"No. Just tired. I need to nap."

"Me, too," Darcy said.

They went inside. Darcy hit the sofa, and Atom headed for the guest stateroom. Bo took the rest of the pitcher back up to the bridge. He turned on some sad country music and sat staring into that turquoise water, drinking and thinking.

About an hour and a half later, Bo heard the door below to the cabin open and then close, and in a few seconds he saw Atom's head as he came up the ladder to the bridge. Bo had finished the pitcher but really didn't feel the alcohol effect. Maybe all that thinking negated all that drinking. Atom was carrying something in his hand.

"I've got something I want you to try," he said. Atom hid the something behind his back as he sat down. "You know fish are attracted to light and you know fish are attracted to colors," he said, adding, "And you also know the ocean is abundant with phosphorus organisms and phosphorescence is an attraction?" Atom stated these truths not as real questions, but as facts he knew Bo already knew, because Bo had shown Atom these things.

Atom reached behind his back and pulled *the something* out, and stuck it in Bo's face, "Voila!"

Bo was looking at a cylindrical object about eight inches long, two inches in diameter, tapered at both ends with a clear plastic tube as the middle. In that clear middle portion was a light green spiral, resembling the old-fashioned red, white and blue barber's pole. The tapered ends ended with stainless steel tips about a half-inch long.

Then Atom, holding it horizontally, grasped each end with one hand, like he was holding a piece of corn. It lit up. The color brightened to a shade of medium to pale green, but what fascinated

Bo was the appearance of depth and florescence. It was not so much a color, but a warm light lime glow.

"What is it, a sex toy?" Bo asked, sarcastically.

"Better than sex to a fish; potential food," Atom replied.

"If I were a fish, I'd eat it," Bo said, even more sarcastically.

"Not eat, son. Attract, attract, attract. Fish will eat just about anything. Attraction is the real sport. Then, once you get their attention, the attraction has to keep attracting as they close in. You want them to get so turned on they'll bite anything, because they just can't help it."

He's right, Bo thought. Lure companies were always sending him free plastic lures to test and promote. The solid plastic heads were always round and ranged from a half inch in diameter to over two inches. The front faces of the heads were flat, sloped, tapered, or bullet-shaped. Depending on the face shape, design, and the speed at which they were pulled, they created all sorts of wakes behind them.

These heads also came in every color a graphics artist had on a color wheel. They had sparkles imbedded in the plastic and eyes; some eyes actually jiggled in their eye sockets, like the eyes on a stuffed teddy bear. Attached to the head was a colorful plastic "skirt" that mimicked the hip-waving motion of a hula dancer's skirt as it swam through the water. The skirt's purpose was to hide the deadly hook underneath. Bo knew all too well that under a lot of skirts, there was a deadly hook.

Bo had never seen one that glowed by itself with a natural ocean phosphorescence, instead of the artificial neon look he was used to.

"Where did you buy this thing?" Bo asked.

Atom's eyes lit up and sparkled with excitement.

"I made it. You're looking at the one, and only one, my boy. It's not meant for day fishing. It's not bright enough. And, as you can see, it's not designed for trolling. I want you to put it down deep, 200 fathoms or deeper, on a wire line and fish at night. Surround it with bottom rigs baited with squid. I believe it will pull creatures you have never seen before from the depths of the sea. Let's see what's really down under in our last frontier."

"I've seen damn near everything that swims or shits in the ocean," Bo said, though not with Atom's same enthusiasm. "But I'll give it shot. What the hell?"

"If it works, I'll give the technology to you, Bo. It might not make you rich, but it could pay a few bills. Just take me fishing once in a while as payment," Atom said smiling.

"Deal. I'll try it, but I'll always take you anyway. You know that," Bo said, thinking he would try anything for money now. He was desperate.

Thud. Darcy hit her head coming up the ladder.

"Good nap, Darcy?" Bo asked. She looked at the lighted glowing lure with the tapered ends.

"What's that?" she asked.

"A new invention of Atom's. A lure," Bo replied.

"It's all lit up. Batteries included?"

"Yes, rechargeable," said Atom.

"Rechargeable ... hmm."

"Let's go eat. I'm starving," Bo announced, afraid of where that was going. "Conch at Angela's Starfish."

CHAPTER 7

They all piled into Bo's ancient World War II vintage Jeep. It really was that old and, remarkably, it really was in World War II. The U.S. Army had brought it over during the war to aid in patrols. The Germans scouted, landed, and even set up camps in the Bahamas. They arrived under cover, and under the ocean surface, in U-boats during the war. The Bahama's close proximity to the United States made the remote islands a strategic jumping off point for espionage.

Bo didn't find the Jeep. The whole island knew it was in the woods, with vines all snaking around, and 40-year old trees growing up through the rusted out floorboards. Bo, was however, the only one to take the initiative and effort to dig it out. Bahamian law says that property abandoned for six months belongs to the finder, so Bo knew he was well within his rights.

Bo and Ratchet, the local mechanic, worked on it, on and off, for over a year to get the thing running. It was Army issue green and had standard five-gallon cans, with holes in them so big they wouldn't hold rocks, strapped on the back bumper, and the long whip antennae growing out of a big spring could be used as a spare fly rod. Bo had wired the antennae to a VHF radio. It even had an old ax in its original slot by the running board. Bo tried to get it out once to kill a snake but 40 years had welded and fused it to the body. Time can either weld two things together permanently, or break them down to dust, thought Bo. It all depends on what the things in question are made of.

The top was down because it didn't have one. Gone as well was the front windshield. Wind was never a problem because the roads were so pocked with potholes that no one could do, or ever did, more than 15 mph. Even if they could or did, the Jeep couldn't; second gear was it and Bo was the only one who could find it. None of the gauges worked, and all the glass covers that were supposed to protect them were shattered. In Bo's mind the Jeep was cherry mint. Bo had named it "U-Boat." He patrolled the waters now, not for Germans, but for fish ... big fish.

They bumped and jogged along down past the old fig tree that was adorned with Christmas tree lights 365 days a year. It wasn't a 365-day celebration of Christ's birthday. Everybody was just too lazy to take the lights down. Could be nobody knew who was supposed to take them down. Whatever, it's the Bahamas. And, hey, if they're there, plug them in.

Right turn, then up the hill to Angela's. Along the way, Bo waved to everybody, and they waved back. He knew almost everybody on the island, and if he didn't, he should. They all knew U-Boat. The screen door to Angela's screeched, waking up Sara.

"Bo, my man, is my big, fat, brown ass gettin' any smaller?" she asked laughing. It was an everyday greeting.

"No, but I like you just the way you are, Sara. You're great, and your ass is as big as your smile," Bo said. It was. She had no recent intentions of ever losing a pound; couldn't. Sara had the biggest butt Bo had ever seen. It was a lot easier to joke about it than face it. When things are beyond hope and repair, maybe it's just easier to joke, give up, and not worry. That's the Bahamian way and maybe the better way.

"To start, Sara, three Kalicks and three orders of conch fritters," Bo said. Kalick is the national Bahamian beer, which is very good, and conch fritters are like hush puppies. They are a kind of meal dough, speckled with diced onion and green and red peppers. They are called conch fritters because bits of conch meat are in the bat-

47

ter. They are deep-fried and served golden brown and hot, right out of the fryer, along with a Thousand Island dressing for dipping.

Bo, Darcy, and Atom took seats in metal folding chairs at the Formica-topped table. Sara brought the beers; the fritters were just starting to fry. The place was very clean and fresh, with a half dozen circulating fans mounted on the ceiling. The walls and ceiling were covered with an assortment of finds: shark jaws with teeth, lacquered turtle shells, seashells, puffer fish and other dead fish, posters and pictures. None of this was placed or designed to create an atmosphere or motif; it was just stuff, just the way it was. The only inconsistencies were the plastic flowers in little vases on the tables. Why plastic, Bo thought, when at arm's length, just outside the door were thousands of flowers? While Sara tended the fritters, Bo and Atom decided on conch burgers. Darcy, on the other hand, wanted two lobsters.

"Hey, that's the most expensive thing on the menu," Bo barked.

"So? You got money. You got that two hundred grand boat, big boy."

"I'm buying. Hush," Atom stated.

Conch burger is served just like a hamburger with all the same accompaniments. Conch meat is the chewy muscle part of the sea snail and has to be beaten with a mallet, like veal; otherwise, you would wear your jaw out with the first bite.

"So, did you snorkel, Darcy?" Bo asked.

"No, I just laid out, then ran, then laid out. I never thought I'd see a beach that pretty."

"You ran? In your flip-flops?"

"No. Yes. No."

"Did you run? Question one."

"Yes."

"Did you wear your flip-flops? Question two."

"No. Why all the questions? What's your fucking problem?"

"I'm glad you had a good time."

Darcy was right about the beach. Bo had seen a lot of beaches in his life, but never one like Briland. He had seen beaches white and powdery as flour, black and coarse as peppercorns, and everything else between. The sand on Briland was pink, not the illusion of pink, but really pink. Out to sea beyond the beach, but close in, were a chain of living reefs from which coral heads grew 30 feet off the sea floor. Many types of coral are red, deep blood red. Over thousands of years, as the coral lived and then died, the open sea fury would break the dead red skeletons away and pulverize them into particles as fine as the sand. The inclusion of this red tint with the natural white sand produced pink. The water at the beach was turquoise and gin clear. The two complimentary colors, pink and turquoise, were dazzling.

"Atom, what is a quark anyway?" Bo asked.

"It's a duck, stupid," Darcy said laughing, but serious.

"Fundamentally, and very basically, it is one of the three energy components of elementary particles assumed to exist as the basic units of all matter. The assumption, aforementioned, is not to assume the pretense that the quark exists or not, but, however, is the total of the energy forces three, and three alone. There could be other sub-quarks or even anti-quarks."

"I got a quark in my neck lying funny on the sand today," Darcy added.

"Relationships of forces, of course, have to ultimately be balanced and they naturally seek, and hopefully find, harmony; otherwise, things will eventually fly apart."

"Harmony. You got that right," Bo agreed.

"Take matter, for example. Could anti-matter exist, if matter didn't exist? Or, could anti-matter possibly be the cause of matter? Yin yang, matter, anti-matter."

"I OD'd on *anti*-biotics one time because I was missin' too much sun from a shitty cold. All it got me was a rip-roaring, yin yang yeast infection." They both looked at Darcy. She had her head down, peeling the label off the beer bottle with her fingernail.

All of a sudden Bo felt sorry for her. She was actually trying to be a part of this conversation. Bless her heart.

"I'm sorry. We'll talk about it later, Atom," Bo said.

"You don't have to be sorry, Bo. I got over it." She didn't even know what Bo was sorry for.

"Hey, let's go see Bulldog and shoot some pool on the way back."

"Deal," Atom said and headed to pay Sara.

CHAPTER 8

Willie's Tavern was a collage of old, one-room structures. As the years went by, the years had meshed, snaked and adjoined walls of every building material imaginable, and some natural walls, like trees, had grown to be a part of the whole. Corrugated metal was actually embedded in trees that had grown folding their trunks around it. Like the ax on the U-Boat, time could weld things together, depending on what it's made of.

Bo had been coming there for years and still got lost finding the bathroom; sometimes it was the maze and sometimes it was *his* daze. Most of the lighting was at table or bar level, not overhead, because in many places there was no overhead to be had. At night you never knew if you had a roof overhead or sky, unless it rained. In fact, one of the only overhead lights was over the pool tables and it hung from a tree limb. As a consequence, the weathering of the pool tables made them extremely challenging. That was to Bulldog's advantage. He knew the dips, valleys, rough spots, smooth spots, and where the sun had hardened the rubber rails. There is not much that can destroy a cue ball, but it had happened at Willie's, twice.

"Atom! How's the psychic world? Read my fortune, Atom, I don't trust these voodoo island folks with *my* future," Bulldog yelled from across the room.

Bulldog never could get the difference between physics and psychic. Really, it's probably the same to most people, all mystic. Bulldog rolled toward Atom, grabbed him, lightning like, and held him up over his head. The sight of the 400-pound bear, and a 100 pounds of that heart, with the nutty professor in the checkered shirt, striped shorts, black socks and sandals, gave comfort and hope to Bo. He thought that maybe he was in the right place and in the right world, after all.

Bulldog set him down and said in his most demanding bass voice, "All right, Doc, am I gonna win this by two balls or five balls or better?"

Losing never entered Bulldog's simple huge head, not in pool or any thing else. He just could not fathom anyone ever meaning him harm or hurt, because he could not, in deeper fathoms, ever harm or hurt anyone else. Win or lose had no real meaning to Bulldog. We all win or we all lose, but if we all do it together, there are no losers or no winners.

Darcy was perched on a barstool, apparently entertaining some locals who were easily entertained by *anybody* they had not grown up with. Bo knew the locals and knew that was all it took, so maybe she could handle it for a while. He settled into a three-quarters empty, orange-colored Naugahyde beanbag wedged into the fork of the same tree that supported the pool table lights to watch the game.

The game was "nine ball." In the Bahamas, rules are stretched and those that can't be remembered are made up on the spot. Nine ball was played by striking the lowest numbered ball on the table with the cue ball. To start the game, break had to be determined, and that ritual was performed by spinning a cut off bill from a blue marlin. Bulldog won.

"You break," Atom announced to Bulldog, who was chalking up his stick.

Tension was building, as well as a crowd. Bo glanced over to check on Darcy. She was fine, had them still enthralled. He wondered if maybe he should find out what had kept their attention that long; they must be stoned. He decided he was comfortable in his seat. The games were about to begin. He stayed put, but only because he could send Chris, his young Bahamian buddy, for another rum and Coke. Bulldog carefully placed the cue ball exactly on an absolute certain spot, as if it really mattered to be just right there. He bent at the waist he didn't have, and his huge belly damn near came to the floor. Bulldog drew back, about to lay into the cue.

"Stop!" yelled Bo. "Twenty bucks on Atom. I'll take all comers."

Bulldog straightened up. "Boss, I hate for you to lose money. You gotta pay me."

Bo looked around and saw the whole crowd digging in their pockets. A cut open yellow gourd hung from a branch near Bo that was used to store the balls, and God knows what else. The money piled in there, and when all takers had tendered their bets, Bo counted the money, $380. Bo matched the bet on a napkin, "*$380 Bo.*" They knew he was good for it.

When everybody resumed their places, Bulldog did too. He reared back and hit the cue ball so hard the crack sounded like an M-16 rifle shot in Laos. Bo's mind flashed. He took a sip of rum and came back. Nine balls and the cue ball jumped, bounced, collided, collided again, for longer than anyone had ever seen. Miraculously, nothing fell. It was unbelievable. Only Bo and Atom grinned. Atom stalked the table like a cat after a bird. He took in every angle, eyeing the situation using his cue stick as guide. The balls had landed in a configuration such that even though Atom had a clean shot at the one ball, it seemed seven others were in the path to the nine ball. The nine lay so temptingly close to the corner pocket. If only Atom could get the one ball to jump over all the other balls and strike the nine, the nine would go in and he would win.

Atom studied the table, then went over to Bo, and they conferred, whispering and pointing. He whipped his mini-turbo computer out of its plastic belt holder and began furiously punching numbers and trig functions. When he was satisfied, he blew across the screen and slipped the computer back into the holder the way a seasoned gunslinger returns his iron to his holster after clearing the smoke. Then they both laughed out loud, and Atom turned back to the table.

"Bulldog, stand over there. You're in my way," Bo shouted.

"I ain't in your way, boss." He wasn't.

"Shit you're not! Stand right there. Now!" Bo shouted, pointing to a spot on the floor. Bulldog always did everything Bo told him. He was the boss, and he always knew best. Bulldog moved to the spot and stood. Atom began to line up his shot.

"Nine ball, corner pocket," he said as he pointed to the corner with his cue stick. Everybody stared quietly, but mumbling, in the background. What Atom was lining up didn't have a prayer. They couldn't figure out what Atom was doing.

"Fat chance," Bulldog said.

"Might oughtin use dat 'puter stead o de stick," another said.

Atom slowly pulled the stick back, took one last correction, and struck the cue ball solidly. The cue ball hit the one ball and rose in the air, off the table surface, and out of the table perimeter. It smacked Bulldog right in the belly. Off Bulldog's belly, it sprung back like it was dropped on a trampoline, landing back on the table and hitting the nine ball perfectly. The nine gently rolled into the pocket. Silence. Then an explosion of laughter and high fives. It was worth the twenty bucks to see it. All agreed ... even Bulldog. Bo got up and emptied the gourd into his own pockets.

"Come on, Atom, Darcy. Let's go back to the boat," Bo said. "Hey, Bull. Don't stay out too late. We're fishin' tomorrow, buddy."

———•———

Back at the boat, they all went in the salon.

"I'm going to bed. I want to be fresh tomorrow," Atom said.

"Me too," Bo said simply. The bed talk got Darcy yawning.

"Me three," she said.

"Three corners?" Atom asked.

"What?"

"Nothing, Darcy, nothing. What about the weather?" Atom asked.

"Five to ten out of the southeast, smooth, no rocky-rolly," Bo answered.

"Great. *You* guys don't rock the boat tonight, okay."

"Good night, Atom. Good night, Darcy," Bo said as he headed to his stateroom.

Darcy was sitting on the sofa, thumbing through a boating magazine. Bo slipped out of his shorts and shirt in seconds and slid into his bed. It wasn't two minutes later his door opened and Darcy came in and did the same thing. Bo didn't know what to think or do. Instinct took over. Bo rolled over to face her, and as he did, he purposely let his hand fall on her boob.

"Look buddy, all I want is a real friggin' bed," she snapped. "Got it, asshole?"

Bo rolled back to his original spot and thought, maybe she is a lesbo *or* this is too much like a brother and sister thing. He closed his eyes and thought about *The Old Man and The Sea*, Bo's favorite book.

CHAPTER 9

Bo was up early; he had gone to bed early. He slid out of bed carefully and slipped into his shorts and shirt. Darcy was asleep, and he left her that way as he went to the head and brushed his teeth and hair.

He had to do an engine room check. Kneeling between the huge engines, Bo checked the fluid levels and the generator. Finally, Bo did a thorough visual and feel. As he moved around he would feel everything, hoses, clamps, belts and filters. This was a necessary ritual. Bo had been in rough seas before when mechanical things failed, and it was no fun. He remembered the time he had to fix a fuel transfer pump in 12- foot seas. The violent motion kept slamming him back and forth between the hot engines; he couldn't use his hands to brace himself because he needed them to perform the task at hand.

When he was satisfied, he jumped back on deck and buttoned up the hatches.

Atom was up by now with the same ridiculous outfit on, minus the shirt.

"Morning, Bo. Everything good to go down there?" Atom asked.

"Yeah, for today, but I've got two cracked cylinder sleeves on the starboard engine. It'll only last a couple of months more, and then I've got to rebuild. Five grand, and I have no way in hell to pay for it. I'll tell you more about the problems on the way out."

"My lure might just be the rescue."

"Yeah, right."

"I'll speak to you later about it. Did you use your lever with Darcy last evening?"

"Lever? Atom, sometimes I just don't get what the hell you're sayin'," Bo said and then thought, Bulldog does. How? "Lever. Oh, that. I just went straight to sleep. Didn't even try. *She* probably wanted to, but she's just gonna have to wait for old Bo here. Character, Atom, character."

"Multi-matrix! You'd fornicate with a fish if it wasn't cold-blooded. Interrupt! I've seen you so cold-blooded it might make a fitting practical protocol."

Bulldog lumbered down the dock, grinning as always.

"What you grinnin' about, buddy?" Bo asked.

"That sure was a good one you pulled last night. You won't trick me again, Boss. Hey, Atom, how ya doin'? Are we gonna catch the momma today?"

Atom pressed his fingers to his temple, closed his eyes and psyched. "We sure as hell are, Bull. I'm as sure as $E=mc^2$."

"I reckon that's pretty sure. You're somethin', Atom," Bulldog said, as he stepped onto the boat. The boat weighed 40,000 pounds, but with Bulldog's weight it went all out of rest and equilibrium like it was offshore in five-foot seas.

Bulldog went about his business getting all the rods out, checking tackle, thawing bait and sharpening hooks. Bo cranked the generator and switched over from shore power to ship power. The generator was not for emergencies. It was sized to run the entire vessel, air conditioning systems, hot water heaters, stove, TVs, lights, everything. The shore power cord was no mere extension cord either. That yellow cord was two inches in diameter, weighed 50 pounds, and was 50 feet long. There were two of them. Bo had unhooked the shore power cords from the boat and was hand-over-hand feeding them to Atom on the dock.

"I wish I could find something to clean these things," said Bo.

"It's like mold feeds and grows on them. I tried every thing advertised, and they're all useless. They just look like big old bananas," he complained. "Oh, by the way, about bananas, you didn't bring any on board, did you?"

"Absolutely negative. I am better educated than that," Atom stated clearly.

If there ever was one thing that is the absolute truth in fishing, it's this: if there are bananas on the boat, you will not catch a fish.

When Bo was doing the tournament circuit, the big joke was to get a case of bananas, then sneak on someone's boat (usually the cockiest sonofabitch's), and shove bananas everywhere. They had put bananas down every rope hawser, every rod holder, every vent, and then hid them in every locker they could get to. It was funny the next morning when the crew came out and saw the "banana bash" that had cursed them sometime in the night. Some laughed at the good nature of the joke and the fact that they had been had and maybe deserved it. Some, however, were so serious about the fishing, they fumed, cussed and made retaliation promises. Regardless of how they took it, they all spent hours scouring the boat to get every last banana off before they left the dock.

Bo remembered one charter trip when it got to be 3 o'clock in the afternoon, and not a lure or bait had been touched all day. The day before he had caught eight dolphin and three tunas. The water condition had improved, and Bo thought the bite that day should be even better. But not one fish. Bo started to wonder.

Half jokingly, he yelled down from the bridge to the charter party in the cockpit, "Y'all didn't bring any bananas on the boat, did you?"

One of the idiots looked up and said, "Yeah, I was going to make banana daiquiris when we got back to the dock."

"Well get those damn things off the boat. You're not going to catch one fish with a banana on board."

They all laughed, and Bo turned forward, thinking, jeeze, what a faggot drink anyway, banana daiquiris. Real men just don't drink daiquiris, much less friggin' banana daiquiris. Bo was getting pissed. He had never, *never* been skunked before. Where the hell are the fish?

Fifteen minutes later and no strike, Bo yelled down again, "You *did* throw those bananas away?"

"No, we thought you were joking."

"Get those bananas off this boat before I come down there and stick every damn one of them up your ass and then throw you over with them."

They realized Bo wasn't kidding and all the smiles melted into looks of concern and even fear. They all just stood there, frozen.

"Shit!" Bo said, as he flipped the autopilot on and swung out of the captain's chair. With one leap he was off the bridge and down in the cockpit. They all scattered to the corners. He went inside the salon and saw a plastic bag of bananas by the sink. He grabbed the bag, ran out in the cockpit and began shaking them out into the water as fast as they would fall. And this is why those guys are still telling the story to this day, and will be telling it to their grandchildren later as well. The second, no, the instant the last banana hit the water, a 80-pound reel popped the rigger and started screaming.

Bo grabbed the guy that brought the bananas by his hair and pulled him to within inches, face to face, like a Marine drill sergeant, and yelled as loud as he never thought he could, "FISH ON, MOTHERFUCKER!!"

Bo slung him towards the chair and headed for the bridge. Although they did catch several fish the rest of the day, the paying party was quite subdued and they didn't tip Bo, or Bulldog either. Bo tipped Bulldog from last night's pool winnings.

———•———

Bo eased *Full Bloom* out of the slip and headed south through the bay created by the west side of Briland and the east tip of North

Eleuthera. It was about two miles wide, but Bo had to go almost to the Eleuthera side to get around a sandbar that extended out from Briland. The sandbar was white, white sand, not like the pink sand on the beach side, and the light reflecting up through the water made it glow azure. The sandbar was home to thousands of huge, red, orange, and yellow starfish. Past the sandbar, Bo headed east out the South Cut for open ocean and the deep blue sea.

Thud. Darcy was coming up the ladder to the bridge. Bo had quit asking if she was all right.

"Hey, you sleep all right?" Bo asked.

"Yeah, I needed it." She took a seat in the companion chair beside the captain's chair, stretched her legs out on the radar box, and rustled her hair.

"Those locals I was talking to last night said they had some home grown island weed that was fuckin' dynamite."

"Well you can do what you want, but don't bring that stuff on this boat. I don't do it, Bulldog don't do it, and I don't want anything to do with it. This is a U.S. Coast Guard documented vessel, and with the zero tolerance crap, they could seize it for nothing more than a seed. And another thing ..."

"All fuckin' right. Don't worry about your little boat. I won't."

They were quiet all the way out to fishing grounds after that, but she didn't go away either. She still sat next to him. Atom and Bulldog were in the cockpit laughing and talking and fiddling with tackle. Bo thought of the yin yang Atom had mentioned. Down there was one of the smartest, most celebrated physicists in the world and the simplest mate, not on the ocean, but on land, carrying on, on an equal level, and truly enjoying each other's company. It made Bo's cold-blooded heart warm.

Six miles off the northeast side of Briland, Bo eased the throttles back and came off plane from running 20 knots to a trolling speed of six to seven knots. Bo knew better than to rely totally on all of *Full Bloom's* fancy electronics. He liked the stuff, but $20,000 worth of electronic navigation gear couldn't even agree on something as simple as speed. The *Full Bloom* had the best knot meter, a duplicate speed meter on the color bottom sounder, Loran, and Global Positioning System (GPS) from satellites. None of them read the same. It didn't matter, really. Bo had been at this game so long that just a look at the wake of the boat and the wave structure behind it, and he could tell within tenths of a knot what was right, and what was not right.

When Bo had backed off to trolling speed, Bulldog and Atom began the business of setting lines out. Darcy decided to lay out. On the forward deck was a bench seat with a four-foot wide cushion. Armed with a towel, the burn oil, and a little cooler of cold beer, she took up residence there.

Bulldog and Atom were working hard, presenting six baits in just the right balanced ballet behind the boat. Bo was trying to stay on the weed line he thought looked promising and figure out its drift. Sargasso weeds often bunched up and interlocked into clumps. Wind and current would string them for miles. Dolphin always feed under them and so do many other species. Trolling around or following the weed line was the best place to fish. Bo periodically cut open the stomachs of the fish just to see what they ate. One time he examined a large dolphin and found 52 seahorses that had been living in the Sargasso weed that morning.

Looking down from his superior vantage point, Bo yelled, "Bulldog, that right outside rigger's too long. It's bouncing funny. Tighten it in ten yards." Bulldog did what he was told.

"Atom, let that short line out a bit." Atom looked up at Bo on the bridge, which meant he wasn't sure which one. It was amazing the communication efficiency a well-oiled team developed after time. Just a slight look or glance or the most subtle idiosyncrasies triggered a response. No words said, just a look, and Atom headed for the right one. A relationship should, if stupid feelings weren't involved, gain and enjoy the same communications. Maybe it did, but a look can be good *or* bad.

When the situation looked right and no more adjustments were in order, Bo climbed up the tower ladder to the tuna tower. A tuna tower is a higher level of platform many feet above the bridge elevation. The higher off the ocean's surface, the farther one could see, and the deeper into the ocean one could see as well. The platform was built of sleek aluminum piping and stylishly raked to complement the boat's lines. The tower has a full set of controls so the boat can be piloted from there as well as from the bridge.

In the beginning, it wasn't so. Pioneers like Hemingway and Rybovich just knew they had to get higher to see and built taller observation platforms out of sticks and plumbing supplies. The tower is still called the "tuna tower" from those same old days when Hemingway needed to spot bluefin tuna cruising by Bimini. He pioneered the structure, and the name has rightfully and respectfully stuck.

Up on the tower Bo studied the baits as much as he thought he ought to, and more than he should. He was supposed to call directives below, but he couldn't find anything wrong, which was unusual. Then he looked forward to stay on that weed line. From the height of the tower he could now see Darcy below, stretched, layin' out on the cushion. She was naked. Nothing. Not even any tan lines or non-tan lines; same difference, no difference. She was brown all over, so Bo guessed, without much guessing, that this had to be her normal way of layin' out.

Bo was mesmerized. Darcy was lying on her back and the massive weight of her breasts had now settled over her ribs. They were so big they had nowhere else to go but to kind of ... puddle, just puddle, right there on her chest. As the boat rocked, her boobs followed gravity, but slowly, just swaying with the movement of the boat. The motion was not sudden or jerky, dampened by their weight. Flip Flop. Tina Turner was wailing *What's Love Got To Do With It* below on the stereo. Bo lost the weed line.

POW! The line exploded out of the left rigger clip.

"Fish on!" Bo yelled as he looked back and down.

Bulldog was already halfway to the rod. He snatched the rod out of the holder and set the hook. Atom was in the chair, ready for Bulldog to hand him the rod. The fish was pulling line off the reel at a good clip, and all Atom could do was hang on and let it happen. In neutral, the boat finally lost its momentum and the reel slowed its screaming accordingly. Bo put the boat in reverse, but only at idle speed. The fish wasn't running now, and he didn't want to back down on more line than Atom could wind. Atom was winding like a machine, it wasn't long until the reel had recovered most of the line it had lost. Bo knew it was too fast and this fish was still very "green" and had a lot of fight left, since he really hadn't expended any real effort yet.

He put the boat in neutral to wait. He did keep the fish directly behind the boat by bumping the engines in and out of gear to keep the alignment right between the boat and fish. This was one of the captain's jobs, and he was good at it. Atom was gaining on him a little at a time. He was a good angler. Raise the rod tip high, then wind on the way down, till the rod was almost parallel to the water. Then ease the rod tip back high again and wind on the way down. This fish wasn't big enough to warrant using his legs to pump. When Atom got the fish to about 100 feet from the boat, the fish saw the boat. Bo was sure the fish now knew something was wrong with this picture and tore off like a bat out of hell. Again, Bo reversed. Atom cranked the reel and they retrieved line. This went on for three more rounds, until the fish was tired. Bo could see the fish now, and the green flashes confirmed what he knew.

"It's a dolphin, nice one," he yelled from above.

The bull dolphin, also known as a dorado or mahi-mahi, is relatively thin with a big forehead, as if it was a round fish that had been run over by an eighteen-wheeler.

A dolphin's color is its spectacular signature. It is bright, bright neon lime green on top, tapering to a just as bright lemon yellow on the sides, and changing to a creamy white coconut on the belly. Sprinkled all over the fish are darker green freckles. Bo always thought the dolphin's colors were the tropics. He hadn't found a place for the freckles yet. Maybe *he* was one of them.

A fish doesn't think. It reacts, like most fishermen, so the dolphin uses the broad flatness of his body to resist. He gets sideways to the direction he is being pulled, like most men. As a result, when a hooked dolphin gets close to the boat, he acts like he is trying to swim around it, when he is only trying to swim away. The captain has to keep the boat in the correct gear to keep the fish somewhat behind the boat for the angler. Before any big dolphin is boated, the boat has probably completed at least full three circles, keeping up with the fish.

This dolphin was true to form, and after *Full Bloom* had followed it for three revolutions, Bulldog had the leader. He eased the fish in, taking only a few feet at a time, while Bo kept a very close eye not to let the fish run underneath the boat. When he had him in range, Bulldog reached out with the gaff and snatched him. The motion was the yin yang of Bulldog's life: like the pool cue - a quick strong extension, and like the gaff - a quick strong retraction. In the same motion, Bulldog hoisted him into the cockpit. He had stuck him good enough to get him in the boat, but when the fish was out of the water he went wild and shook off the gaff.

A dolphin loose in the cockpit is dangerous. The long tail slaps and whips fiercely. Bo had seen many customers not quick enough to get out of the way, go home with huge welts on their legs.

Bulldog stalked him and waited, out of the danger zone, until his flipping and flapping would land him in a position that presented his head. Bulldog was instinctual when it came to handling fish. He was patient and waited, and when he got a clear shot, WHAM! One clean shot in the head with the wooden bat and the fish hushed. Flip Flop.

Bulldog high fived it with Atom, whooped it up, holding dinner just as high. Then he slid him across the deck into the fish box, where the ice waited. Once the box lid was down, seriousness resumed as quickly as it had erupted into triumph, and act two was on stage. The whole process began all over again.

"Get the baits back out," Bo yelled, as he turned forward trying to find another weed line. Atom and Bull were good in the cockpit and the *Full Bloom* was hunting again in minutes.

Darcy, meanwhile, was oblivious to all the action, lying peacefully in homage to the "sun god."

Searching, Bo sighted some bait boiling the water about a quarter mile at 120 degrees. He pointed the boat towards them. As he was closing in, the bait fish dived, but Bo knew they were still headed northeast. He overran them and then circled back to school them, knowing they would be confused. Confusion creates opportunity. Pulling his baits through where he knew the school was, the longest line he had out popped, and the reel screamed.

"Fish on! Tuna! I guarantee it!" Bo hollered below. This fish ran, ran, ran, and then ran some more, peeling off several hundred yards of line. Then it stopped. Bo backed down. As Bo backed down, Atom kept up, but the angle of the line in the water became more downward. The fish had dived, which wasn't unusual for tunas. When the line was tight and straight down, Bo knew it was just a waiting game. He took the opportunity and clambered down from the tower to the cockpit and announced, "I got to take a whiz," and went inside.

On the way out, he opened a drawer that stored his stash of beef jerky, M&M's, cheese crackers, Snickers and beef jerky again, kind of layered. All this he bought at a commercial wholesale house, so the stash came in boxes labeled four dozen gross, minimum. He grabbed crackers and M&M's, lunch and dessert in one trip.

Out in the cockpit, Atom just sat holding on, as the fish just sat holding on. Bulldog was tending to him, but nothing needed tending to. Tuna will do that. They're frustrating, Bo thought. That's why we eat them raw, sushi. It was primeval. Give me a hard time and I won't even bother cooking you before I eat you.

"All right, let's get him up," Bo said.

"How?" Atom asked.

"I gotta trick."

"Do it. I'm tired."

Bo went over to the line, straight down and tight as a banjo string. Bulldog moseyed over too, knowing the tuna trick and taking the cue. Bo plucked the line in the rhythm of *Old Man River* and began to sing the tune. Bulldog had an operatic voice and chorused in immediately, drowning out Bo, "Old man river, that old man river, he just keeps rolling aloooong."

"What the expanded notation are you doing?" Atom quizzed.

"Tunas hate that song." The tuna began to rise and the line rose with him.

"I don't believe this, this theorem," Atom said.

"See, Atom, there are some things *I* know and you don't know. Figure that one out, Mr. Scientist."

Bulldog was still singing.

"That's enough, Bull. He got the message."

Bo leaped to the bridge to take control of the boat. As the line's angle to the surface rose more, Bo backed down and Atom cranked. A few minutes later, Bull nailed the fish with the gaff, and sushi was on the menu. Bulldog whipped out his knife, and with one whack chopped his tail off and with another whack took a pectoral fin. He then placed the tuna, finless side down, on the ice in the fish box. This was to bleed him. Tunas build up toxins if they are not bled immediately, and fine sushi would become just a grilled steak.

Atom was awestruck. Bo knew his mind was in hyper-gear trying to make sense of the trick. He was waiting for Atom to un-holster his computer and start punching numbers. Atom couldn't stand to not understand.

"All right Atom, I'll tell you," Bo finally said. "It's not the singing or the song. The fish felt the reverberations of me plucking the line. He already knew he didn't like what was in his mouth. But to have it thumping, too, drove him crazy. He had to do something, and up was the only way to go."

"You never told me that. You always said they hated my singing," Bulldog said.

"You sing great, Bull. Don't stop."

Bulldog started singing again.

"I don't mean *now*. Just the next time, big guy."

It was noon by then, and all the baits were perfect. Bo knew it didn't matter; fish never hit at lunchtime. They never did. It was strange. When humans are supposed to be hungry and eat, fish won't. Maybe it was a game, or maybe they were just mighty considerate.

Darcy was as considerate as the fish. When she eased around the side of the boat and jumped into the cockpit, she had put on her suit. Now that was considerate, although nobody really appreciated it. Or again, maybe it's all a game.

"I'm starving. You got any friggin' food on this boat?" She demanded.

"M&Ms, beef jerky, cheese crackers," Bo said from the bridge.

"That ain't food."

"Peanut butter and jelly in the fridge."

"That's what I need, calories." She really meant it. "Where's the bread?"

"In the locker, left of the sink. Make me one, too. Ten roger?"

"If you've got enough, me too," Atom said.

"I'll fix you one, Atom, but Bo, just 'cause I told you I was a professional server don't mean I'm here to serve up *your* shit."

"I'll let you have sex with me."

"Sex with you! Buddy Bo, that would be about as much fun as

watching a macaroni bush grow." Darcy headed in.

"What?" Bo and Atom chorused in unison, shaking their heads. Even Bulldog looked perplexed.

Atom came up the ladder to the bridge from the cockpit and took the companion chair next to the captain's chair. He propped his white legs up on the tower structure and toward the most sun. Bulldog was still in the cockpit, sharpening hooks and just generally piddling. It was that slow time of the day.

"How's Julia?" Bo asked. Atom's niece, Julia, had leukemia and was at Egleston Children's Hospital in Atlanta.

"She's holding her own, bless her heart. It doesn't look good though."

"Damn. I hate to hear that."

Julia was eight now, and Atom had first brought her down when she was six. Bo had paraded her around the island like she was his own. They had hit the beach running and rode horses in the water. Together, they sat on the sand talking and watching the tide melt the sand castles they had made. On the bay side, they swam and snorkeled over the starfish, exploring.

Bo taught her the slowest race in the world. Each would pick a starfish to bet on. In shallow water they would turn them over on their backs at the same time. The starfish instinctually had to right themselves by digging two of the five points into the sand as anchors. By moving water around in various internal chambers, the starfish would fold in half with one point straight up. As they folded more, one point would come over, like a gymnast puts her legs behind her head. Then they would flatten out in the right position, face down. The race didn't keep them on the edge of their seats, since the whole process took about ten minutes. For some reason Julia's starfish usually won.

The highlight of Julia's trip came when Bo had taken her to the hair salon. Throughout the Caribbean the girls braided their hair in tiny cornrows, culminating on the ends with multicolored beads.

The beads snapped and crackled against each other when she turned her head. The last time he had talked to her, he had promised to take her to get the "beads" again.

Bo never knew he liked children until Julia, but he was crazy about her. He enjoyed Julia's innocence. Bo hadn't been around much innocence in life, especially his own. Maybe he was hoping some of it would return; but he knew it couldn't, it was gone forever. He couldn't cry over spilled guts.

"Grub's up," Darcy announced, coming out of the cabin holding sandwiches wrapped in paper towels high above her head to reach to the bridge.

"The crust's on. I can't eat it," Bo said.

She didn't say a thing. Darcy grabbed the knife Bulldog had been cutting and trimming bait with all day. On the same cutting board Bulldog had been using, she neatly sliced the crust away. What she handed back was a crustless sandwich sopped with squid ink and bits of tentacles dripping from the edges.

"Eat every fuckin' bite or I'll use this knife to cut your crust off next."

Bo ate. With his mouth half full he put *Full Bloom* into neutral. Bo yelled to Bulldog,

"The bite's back on. It's 1:30; action time coming up. Let's get 'em in and put out the magic."

Bo threw the rest of his sandwich way off the boat where Darcy couldn't see and clambered down to get the bonefish out of the fridge and to help Bulldog get them under tow. Bo was hunting for the big blue marlin momma now. He and Bulldog put out four bonefish on 80-pound reels. Two were on the outside riggers, way back, and two were on the inside, about middle range. In addition, Bo towed two teasers inside, ten yards in front of the two inside baits. Teasers were big-headed, plastic lures with long skirts but no hooks underneath. Their purpose was to create a lot of commotion in the water to draw the big blues from down deep to check out what the hell was going on.

Darcy re-took her position on the bow seat. Atom was in the fighting chair, ready, and Bulldog stared at the baits from the cockpit, poised to pounce in a second. Bo was at the bridge controls, pointing the boat toward some bottom he knew had deep canyons and hills. Using binoculars, Bo spotted the water boiling with a school of bonito, about a mile off. There had to be three acres of them. Birds hovered, darted, and dipped over the bonito following the same feeding frenzy as the fish. Bo cut his radar on and picked up the birds painting a blob on the screen. By watching the mass on the radar screen, he could determine the direction of the party. He pointed the boat to intercept.

As he neared, Bo positioned the boat ahead of them and the whole mass turned in unison. Really, the fish turned away, and the birds followed. Bo throttled up a knot and began circling, keeping them corralled and bunched up. He was sure there had to be some big blues trying to feed in there.

Bo was right. Sure enough, on the second circle, POW! Zzzzzzzzzz! The left long line was hit, and the reel screamed.

"Fish on!" Bo hollered, like nobody knew. It was just years of reaction.

Bulldog was on it, again, lightning like. He yanked the rod out of the holder and got it to the chair, where Atom was ready. All Atom could do was just hold on as the big fish stripped line from the reel. With the same fluid speed, Bulldog was winding in the other reels like a machine. The fat man was amazing. He could wind a reel like an electric motor. Bo was getting the teasers in almost as fast from the bridge. Once done, this cleared the whole field for the anticipated fight.

Two hundred yards back, the big blue started greyhound leaping so frantically she was going end over end, bill over tail. Line was peeling steady and strong. At a half of spool left on the reel, she was out 800 yards. For the whole run, Atom had kept the drag hard on, trying to stop her, and the reel had begun to smell and smoke like squealing tires.

"Loosen up the drag, Atom," Bo yelled. "Get some ice on that reel, Bull."

Bulldog filled a plastic bag full of ice water and held it against the reel. Bo was backing down hard. Water was splashing over the transom, as if a fountain were in the cockpit. The big diesels roared, and the rudders rattled. Boats were not designed to go backwards at that speed. With a quarter spool left, the big fish decided to take a breather. Bo didn't let off, though. He had to help Atom recover some line. Atom did, too. He wound like hell. It took 30 minutes to get her to within 50 yards. Now Bo wanted to ease back very gently so as to not spook her. Little by little, Atom cranked. This fish let the boat back down to her so close that Bulldog could grab the leader and he did. Bo knew a fish that big was in no way ready for the end. As soon as Bulldog touched the leader, she shot straight out of the water, clearing the surface by 15 feet.

She was a *grander*, over 1,000 pounds and 12 feet long, not counting the bill. The blue on her back was pulsing and psyche delic, with lighter blue neon stripes running down her sides. She came down with a splash, like an exploding cannonball, soaking the whole boat. This was war! Seconds later, she surfaced again, pissed off, and tail-walked a good 30 feet. She shook her head, daring them all and staring at them all through an eye as big as a softball.

"Yeehaa! Ride her, Atom!" Bo was screaming.

"WOO, WOO, WOO, ...WOO!" Bulldog was chanting. Zzzzzzzz! She took off faster than Bo had ever seen a fish go before.

Atom strained, but could do nothing except hang on; his butt lifted three inches off the seat and just hung there from the pull. The reel started smoking from heat and making loud grating noises.

"Bull, that reel's gonna go. Get another one on, pronto," Bo yelled.

Bulldog was on the way and snatched up another 80-pound rig. Bo was watching.

"Don't clip the new line to the top of the reel; clip it to base of the reel by the rod, Bull."

That was quick thinking. As soon as Bulldog secured the new line, the reel exploded and parts of it flew all over the cockpit like hot shrapnel. Bulldog yanked the old rod with the destroyed reel out of the chair, threw the whole mess over the transom with one hand, and with the other stuck the new one in Atom's face.

"Here ya' go. A brand new one just for you, cause you my 'lil buddy, Atom." Bulldog was proud.

"Great work, Bull. Great work, big guy," Bo called down.

The fish was stripping line off the new one so fast Bo was worried she wouldn't stop. Atom held on, suspended in his crouched position, like a jockey riding a thoroughbred.

Darcy slipped around the side and jumped into the cockpit, with no top on.

"What the hell's going on back here?" No one seemed to notice the huge boobs that swung all over, making dancing shadows on the cockpit deck. If any of the three guys did, they certainly didn't care. Priorities are priorities.

"We're fishing. Man, are we fishing big time!" Bo yelled to her as he revved the big diesels in reverse. An hour had gone by since the strike and Atom was sweating his ass off.

"My thermal situation is reaching critical. Assist me." Atom strained to get his words out.

"What he say, Boss?" Bulldog yelled to Bo.

"He's hot as hell, Bull!"

"No problem, Mon," Bulldog responded and went for the hose.

"Darcy, grab that bag of ice and hold it against that reel. Show her where, Bull," Bo yelled.

As Bulldog hosed Atom he showed Darcy where to hold the ice pack on the reel. The boat rocked, and she was forced to let the pack come on and off the reel. It sizzled every time she reconnected. Bo had the boat in reverse, faster than he ever had. Seawater was pouring over the transom more quickly than it could escape through the draining scuppers. Darcy and Bulldog were standing on either side of the chair tending Atom and didn't even notice they were in a foot of water.

Bo did notice, and had to slow up. If he let too much water in, the weight would continue to push the stern deeper into the ocean, which could be a big problem. He waited and timed to allow enough water to drain before he poured it to the big diesels again. With only a 100 yards left on the second reel, she stopped. Bo kept up and the line went slack, the first they had seen with this fish.

"Wind, Atom! Wind, Atom! Wind, wind, wind!" Bo screamed.

" I can't, man. I just can't." Atom's arms were cramped and he felt like they had been pulled out of his shoulder sockets.

"We'll lose the sonofabitch, Atom! Wind!"

"My appendages are becoming inoperable."

"That fish cost me a thousand dollar reel and, by God, I'm gonna get her. If I let Bull touch that reel, the IGFA ain't gonna recognize nothin'."

"What if I did it, Bo?" Darcy asked.

"Thanks, but that's not the point, sweetheart."

The International Game Fish Association, IGFA, rules state if anyone touches the gear, rod, or reel to help in any way before the leader is secured, the fish is disqualified.

"I want to, but ... but my arms won't operate, Bo. I simply cannot."

"Damn. Okay, Bull, do it. At least we can say the *boat* caught her. We've got to get the other rod back anyway."

Atom still sat in the chair with his paralyzed arms stretched to beyond max, while Bulldog stood beside and cranked the reel. The fish was a mile and a half away. It took forty-five minutes to reach her. She was spent. She was lying exhausted from that last run, the likes of which Bo had never seen before. Bo was worried she was dead from the way she floated gently on her side. That God-given brilliant color had turned dull gray and mottled, and there was no movement of her gill plates.

Full Bloom eased back, and Bulldog rolled over the transom and stood on the swim platform. The big man with the giant hands used one to grasp the bill and the other to pull the hook out. The bill was as big around as a slugger's baseball bat, the business end. When Bulldog yanked the hook, she twitched her fin and gave a slight slap of her tail.

"She's alive!" Bo yelled. "Get her, Bull!"

Bulldog held the bill and came across the transom back into the cockpit. Over the side and bent double, a definite illusion, Bulldog then grabbed the bill in both hands and forced the fish as far down in the water as he could stretch. Bo put the boat in gear at idle speed and began to move forward. Any man less than 400 pounds could not have held that fish and stayed in the cockpit. Water was being forced to wash over her gills. This was fish resuscitation. She needed to expend no energy, but was getting more than she needed in oxygen.

For ten minutes, Bulldog just held on, while everybody was silent, watching the fish and the crack of Bulldog's huge bent-over ass, all in the same picture. She started a slow swish of her tail, and her color was returning.

"Bull, it's still too early. Can you hang on?" Bo said.

"Why my name Bulldog, Boss?"

"You da man."

After another ten minutes, all her color was back. She was actually starting to fight with Bulldog to get away.

"I do believe she's back, Bull. Turn her loose."

As he did, she glided away from the boat, pectoral fins straight out like an albatross cruising the currents. She had a tired but strong kick, and Bo felt she was going to make it.

Bo flipped the boat on autopilot, swung down from the bridge, and whooped it up, high fiving it with Bulldog. Atom couldn't high five; his arms couldn't move. So Bulldog just gave him a bear hug. Bo hugged Darcy. He stepped back, and, holding her hands in his, he started a jig that she couldn't follow, but had to try. Bo was pumping her arms back and forth in a way that made her boobs bounce and rotate in opposite directions. Flip Flop. Everybody howled and laughed but none any louder than Darcy. She was a sport.

"Get the rum jug, Darcy," Bo shouted. "We're headed for the hill."

Bo got *Full Bloom* up on plane and headed toward the South Cut, letting the big dog eat, or slurp, diesel fuel. Bulldog took his usual position and melted into a massive blob on the cockpit deck, in the center, as was Bo's rule. Atom took the companion chair, and Darcy was immediately in front of Bo on the bench seat. When running hard, it was too loud to carry on a conversation, so they sat and rode and passed the rum, drinking it straight out of the bottle. Each was absorbed in his or her own world and thoughts, which, with these three souls, had to be very different.

By the time Bo turned into the marina, everybody was asleep. Bo, too, almost. The rocking of the boat, the sun, the work, and the excitement had worn everybody slap out. The rum had pulled the plug completely. He bent over the bridge rail and poured the last of the rum on Bulldog to wake him up so he could help with the lines. The rum dribble didn't work, and Bo considered throwing the bottle at him, but worried if he hit Bulldog's head he would have to contend with tiny glass slivers finding ways into his feet for months.

Bo backed *Full Bloom* into her slip and because there was no wind, he could come off the bridge and secure the boat himself. Then he went back up to the bridge, popped in a Patsy Cline tape and played, "Crazy, crazy for loving you ..." at max volume.

"Get that honky-tonk shit outta my face!" Darcy yelled, and then laid back with her hands over her ears.

"Explosion in the lab!" Atom yelled, startled into sitting up.

Only Bulldog smiled as he slowly got up and said, "I like her. Ain't that Kathy Cline?"

"Patsy."

"I ain't no patsy just 'cause I like her music, Boss."

Bo turned the stereo off. Patsy had done her job.

"Get the fish out of the box and clean 'em. Then clean the fish boxes, and that's all we're gonna do tonight. We'll get Leslie and Cliff to give her a good bath in the morning."

"I can't get down the ladder. My arms don't work," Atom complained halfway down.

"I'll help you, lil' buddy," Bulldog went to assist. The big man picked him up and carried him all the way to his bunk. When he came back out, he yanked the fish box out of the cockpit deck, and with one and the same motion slung it on the dock. With ice and fish, it was a mere 300 pounds.

"Bull, I'm going to bed, too. Put the fish in the dock refrigerator. Thanks, buddy. See you in the morning," Bo said as went up to the bridge to cut off all the electronics.

He helped Darcy up, but she was still half asleep and he had to struggle to get her down the ladder and into the cabin to bed, her final resting place, for the night anyway. After one quick check of the ship's systems, Bo shucked his clothes and climbed in with her. Absolutely nothing was on his mind, and as he closed his eyes he realized, *nothing* was on his mind. This *is* becoming a brother and sister thing, with a lesbian for a sister, no less.

CHAPTER 10

Bo woke early. He felt great, but he always had been a morning person. Somehow, and luckily so, he had the ability to cleanse himself of his problems and filter the alcohol overnight then he could truly look at a new day as truly, a new day. He glanced over at Darcy sleeping peacefully. He didn't even try anything. He felt good enough already, why chance it?

A better pair of shorts and an official *Full Bloom* monogrammed golf shirt were the order of the day, since he was going to accompany Atom to the airport. Charging twelve hundred bucks a day for fishing, Bo figured, sometimes he had to *look* professional, at least when out, and especially off the island. Carrying a quick cup of coffee, he emerged from the cabin and into the cockpit. The eastern side of North Eleuthera was just greening up from the rising sun. As he sat on the covering boards counting his live baits in the wire pen, he made a face at the barracudas.

"Pieces of crap," he muttered. The barracudas were motionless, except for the tiny motion of their fins to keep them in place. They just hung there, lurking and skulking. Bo felt too good that morning to let them live. He went in and, groping under the sofa, retrieved his spear. The spear was a five-foot long slender, stainless steel rod sharpened to a razor point with a retractable barb. On the butt end, the rod had a hole to attach a retrieval line.

Bo threaded a 50-pound line through and cinched it. He leaned over the side of the boat, bracing himself with his thighs against the combing padding. Gripping the spear, not like Cro-Magnon man with the whole hand, but delicately with a few fingers and thumb, he poised and aimed. Checking the security of his anchoring on the deck, he twisted on the balls of his feet like a batter digging in his cleats in the batter box. He knew he was going to put his whole body into the only chance he would have, and he didn't want to follow the spear and get saltwater on the only clean clothes he had.

Rechecking his aim, he was ready. Both eyes open now. Never throw spears without both eyes open. Never. Deep breath and ... whoosh! The stainless sparkled, and the tip pierced the water without even a ripple. All of a sudden, the plastic spool holding the retrieval line spun out of control, spinning and skipping and dancing all over the cockpit like a runaway yo-yo. Bo dove for it, chasing it, and missing it, then chasing it again. A loop of the frantic line wrapped around his big toe and came tight.

"Gotcha, 'cuda, gotcha, gotcha, gotcha!" he yelled as he grabbed at his foot. He took two wraps of the line in his hand, ready to do battle, and then the line went limp.

"Son of a ... !" Bo began to gather the line to get his spear back. When the butt end of the spear reached him, he grabbed it, but it was heavy. He looked down.

"Damn, I'm good, *real* good," he said to himself. That ten-pound 'cuda was violently penetrated right through his tiny ass heart. Bo flung him on the deck with the spear still in him, and he stood up proud with the butt of the spear in his left hand. The cabin door opened.

"Morning, Poseidon," Atom said. "I'll tell you, you men of the sea are really something. However, I regret to inform you, that you are not quite Poseidon; that spear's in the wrong hand."

Bo quickly changed hands.

"Too late, my man. You're just a lowly 'cuda slayer," Atom laughed. Bo grinned. Blood flowed on the deck.

"Cap'n Bo, Cap'n Bo, can I have him, can I?" Leslie, a cute little ten-year-old Bahamian boy on the dock begged.

"Sure, Leslie," Bo said flinging the mess up on the dock. "But you got to clean my spear, and bring it back polished, too. Ten, roger?"

"Ten roger!"

Nobody ate barracuda. The meat was awful, but the islanders did a pretty good job smoking them, and that made the flesh at least tolerable table fare.

"Let's get some more coffee," Bo said, as they went back into the cabin.

"We got to get your gear packed and over to the airport if you're going to catch the 9 o'clock to Nassau."

"I know. I've been at it some, but my arms aren't in the best of shape."

"Suck it up, scientist."

Darcy came stumbling out of the stateroom. Bo thought, she was no morning person.

"Gimme some coffee," she demanded.

"Please?"

"Fuck you," she shot back.

No doubt about it now, she definitely was not a morning person.

"You should have witnessed Poseidon here this morning, Darcy," Atom said.

"I know he's a piss-ant. Where's the damn coffee?"

Bo and Atom just looked at each other, and then shook their heads in amazement.

———•———

"It's 8:15. Come on, Darcy. He'll miss the plane," Bo called into the cabin from his tender, *The Bud*. *The Bud* was a 16-foot skiff with a 40-horsepower outboard motor that was the official tender to *Full Bloom*. Bo was at the wheel, and Atom sat on the middle bench with his trusty, avocado green Samsonite suitcase tucked under his arm like a big puppy.

"I can't find my flip-flops," Darcy yelled.

"Good! Come on."

She clambered over the covering boards and plopped down in the bow seat, facing Bo and Atom. Bo backed out of the marina and was idling past the other boats.

"I've never been to an airport in a boat," Darcy said. "In fact, I've never been to an airport."

"Well, don't use this airport as your measuring stick, Darcy," Bo said. "We are going to run across the bay to the dock, right over there," he said, pointing. "From the dock we'll catch a cab up the hill about two miles to the North Eleuthera Airport."

Upon reaching Three Island Dock, Bo secured *The Bud* to some old cleats and they all jumped into a cab. Now, cabs in the Out Islands were not like cabs in the States. Most of them were old station wagons discarded from Florida. The springs were mush from pot-holed roads and shocks were nonexistent from lack of parts. The tropic sun had also taken its toll. Paint peeled, as did vinyl tops and plastic parts, all peeling and curling under that hot tropic sun. The common color was rust. The seats were on at least the third slip cover, or that was as many layers as a brave man dared to count, scared to dig any deeper. The headliners were always stuck in place with hundreds of multi-colored pins. It looked like a strategic business map with a pin marking every WalMart location. The main difference between stateside cabs and Out Island cabs was that the drivers were always pleasant and helpful. They had their dignity, too; they always wore ties. Bo would rather take an ox cart with a good guy at the reins than a limo with an asshole at the wheel.

"Morning, Mr. Sawyer," Bo greeted the first cab driver.

"Mornin', Cap'n Bo. How are you on this glorious mornin'?" Mr. Sawyer asked.

"We're just great! Except my friend here has to go back. How's your family?"

"Da Lawd jus' bless me with my sixth granchile last week. Praise da Lawd."

"Terrific, a boy or a girl?"

"Girl, a precious li'l girl."

"Well, she couldn't have a better grandpappy."

"Bless you, Bo, and you friends."

"Well, you're a good friend too, Mr. Sawyer."

Bo liked these people; they were real in an unreal world out here in these Out Islands, or maybe out here was the real world and they were unreal.

"Puleeeze. Why don't y'all just kiss for Christ's sake," Darcy said as she popped up in the back.

"Hush," Atom said to Darcy, rapping her on her knee. "They're just trying to be nice."

Mr. Sawyer had heard. "Naw, Mam, we ain't tryin' to be nice - we *genuine* nice. Right, Bo?"

"Right you are, Mr. Sawyer; so right you are." He really liked these people.

Darcy hushed.

Mr. Sawyer rolled his wagon up the curb gently, wiggled the shift into park, and got out to help with the bag.

Bo got his money out. "How much we owe you today, Mr. Sawyer?" Bo knew how much, but it was polite to ask.

"That'll be twelve dollar today, Cap'n Bo."

Bo peeled off the money and added a couple for tip.

"Let me see that," Darcy said, grabbing for Bo's wad.

"What?"

"That's money?"

"Bahamian money."

"Looks like play money."

"All money would be play money to you, Darcy." He let her have some.

Bo marveled at Bahamian money. The colors were bright

blues, greens, pinks, yellows, and reds. The bills sported boating scenes, beach scenes, underwater reef scenes, and maps. The Queen of England's face was on all of them, smiling radiantly in crown and jewels. Sandollars punctuated important parts, like the value of the bill. Maybe Darcy was right. It was play money, or at least happy money. All money ought to be happy money and Bo would be very *happy* if he had some.

"Hold it up to the light."

"What light?"

"Just hold it up toward the sky and look right here," Bo said as he pointed to a blank spot on the bill.

"Looks like some crosses on some sails."

"Good, Darcy. That's right. It's called a watermark. Those are the sails on the Santa Maria, Christopher Columbus' boat. He first landed on the Bahamian island of San Salvador, south of here."

"I've heard of Christopher Columbus."

"Good for you. Now you've seen a picture of his boat."

North Eleuthera airport is a small, yellow, single-story, masonry building. There are two sides which cater to essentially the "coming and going." The coming, or arrival, side houses immigration and customs. It has metal tables for bag inspection and no chairs because they want you out of there. The going, or departure side, has rows of cheap plastic bucket seats of all colors facing long ticket counters, because they want you out of there, too. But, it doesn't work that way in the Bahamas, and you could end up living there forever. At the little corner bar, a rum and Coke is only $2.

Atom turned in his paperwork and took a seat and Bo sat down beside him. Darcy found the little bar and a use for the play money Bo had given her.

"Flying BahamasAir is always an experience," Atom said.

"I know. They've got nothing newer than Korean War vintage. It's kind of nostalgic; it takes you back in time."

"I just want to *get* back," Atom declared.

"It's strange. All those planes are damn near held together with duct tape, and they have the best record in aviation. Never lost one."

"Say not?"

"It's true."

"Look, I want you to promise me you will try that lure. I want it down deep and at night. You promise?" Atom was stern.

"I promise. I promise."

"Think about it, Bo. All the fishing you do is identical to what everybody else typically does, pulling surface baits, the same baits, the same lures, the same apparatus all over the world. Nobody's trying down in the depths, deep with illumination. I just know there's curious life down there we have never seen heretofore."

"Yeah, Atom, but who wants to crank in some big ol' fish, when you can play one dancing before your eyes, glittering in the sunlight? That's sport. What you're talking about is damn near commercial meat fishing."

"Very well, return the lure back to my address at Tech, post haste."

"No, no, no. I didn't mean that, but I'm a sport fisherman, not a meat guy."

"Where's your sense of adventure and discovery, Bo? That's not characteristic of you."

"I've got enough adventure trying to keep my boat running. As for discovery, I need to discover some money real friggin' bad."

"Do it."

"I will."

"When?"

"Soon."

"When?"

"Soon, Atom."

"When?"

"Tonight! Goddammit!"

"Shake."

Bo shook his friend's hand and yelled as Atom was headed to the door.

"Tight lines to ya!"

The plane, with all six seats, was taxiing up and the noise made further conversation impossible. Thank God, Bo thought. He didn't want to talk about it anymore. He had made a promise and he kept his promises. Uh-oh, he thought at first the noise was his savior, but now he couldn't talk his way out of it. Atom was almost out the door. He waved at Bo and then at Darcy, and then was gone. The plane swung around, headed for the runway, and as it did, it blew all the paperwork on the counters everywhere. The nice ladies, who were the gate attendants, scrambled and cursed under their breath very politely.

Bo and Darcy took Mr. Thompson's cab back this time.

"How's the family, Mr. Thompson?"

"Fine Cap'n Bo. Thanks so very much fo' askin'. Da Lawd jus bless me and da wife wid anudda chil' last week ..."

The car rumbled on down the hill towards Three Island Dock.

CHAPTER 11

As Bo rounded the corner into the marina, he could see Leslie and Cliff finishing the chamois job on *Full Bloom*. Bulldog was in the cockpit cleaning all the tackle and rods and reels.

"Good job, guys," Bo called out.

"Mornin', Boss."

"Jeeze, it's pretty. I want to lay out," Darcy said.

"Have at it." Darcy had found a home, or better, an altar, on the bow bench.

"Bull, Atom made me promise to try some lure he invented. Problem is he got me to promise to do it tonight, and he slipped away before I could weasel out of it."

Bulldog puzzled, "What we gonna catch at night, Boss? We don't fish at night."

"The lure lights up. It's battery powered. Atom wants it down deep. I guess we'll put it on a wire line with the big electric."

Bo had a rod and reel that's whole spool was wire instead of regular monofilament line. It was extremely strong and had no stretch. Attached to the reel was an electric starter motor that came out of a small car that, with a flick of a switch, would wind the wire. Anyone who tried to wind a hundred fathoms of wire with a three-pound weight on the end, would have their arm fall off before the job was halfway done.

"I better check out the electric. We ain't used it in a year."

"Good thinking, Bull."

"You know that spot about eight miles off the South Cut, at

about 110 degrees?"

"Yeah?" Bulldog didn't know.

"It's almost due east of the Glass Window. It's that place where the bottom sounder always picked up swirls of color from at least 200 fathoms. It kinda looked like a fire in the water, way down. But then the colors just disappeared. Remember how it started out real red and purple, then went to yellow and green, and then just melted into blue?"

"Yeah, yeah. We thought it was weird bait, but bait don't swim like that," Bulldog said.

"You got it. That's where we'll try the damn thing. I saved the numbers on it," Bo said, referring to the latitude/longitude coordinates.

"Night fishin'. Shit, Boss."

"I know. I know, Bull. But I'm gonna keep my promise. It'll just be this one friggin' time."

Bulldog checked the electric; then he left to cut his grass. Bo reviewed his charts and re-read *The Old Man and the Sea* for the zillionth time. Darcy worshipped the sun god. It was a lazy afternoon in paradise.

After they had cheeseburgers at the bar, the sun ducked under North Eleuthera across the bay to the west. Bulldog came around the corner.

"Hey, Boss. Let's get this stuff over. I got a game at 11 o'clock. Dude's got $50 on the table."

"All right, Bull. Go get the generator started. I'll be right down."

"Where we goin', Buddy Bo?" Darcy asked in good spirits. The sun god had smiled on her that day.

"Night fishing with Atom's lure invention. Remember the one you thought was a sex toy?"

"You mean with the rechargeable batteries?"

"Yeah," Bo said, unenthusiastically.

"Fishy, fishy, fishy," Darcy said, smiling mysteriously.

"What in the hell are you talking about? Sandy, let me sign. Let's go."

At night the bridge of the *Full Bloom* looked like the bridge on a battleship. The panel lights twinkled while the radar cast an eerie green glow. Blue came from the depth sounder, yellow from the GPS charting plotter, and an assortment of reds came from indicator lights on the VHF radio, single-side band radio, synchronizers and a slew of other instruments. It was like standing in front of a jukebox.

Bo maneuvered the boat around the south starfish sandbar, guided by the lights from a house on North Eleuthera, his depth sounder, and the GPS charting plotter, which tracked every move. Once safely out the South Cut, he powered up and set the autopilot on 110 degrees. The plotter would sound an audible beep when the boat got close to the destination.

"Darcy, would you mind getting us some rum and Cokes?" Bo asked. "Squeeze some limes in them, too; they're in the refrigerator."

"No problem, mon. I am a professional server, you know."

"You're mighty agreeable tonight," said Bo.

"I know, sweetheart," she said over her shoulder as she headed below.

God, it is pretty out here, Bo thought. The lights of the islands didn't fade because of distance, but because of the curvature of the earth. They fell below the horizon, like the moon or sun setting. The moon was a new moon, so there wasn't any moon. Bo dimmed all the lights from his instruments and navigational gear. With all the light pollution gone, the stars appeared brighter than ever. As Atom always said, the physical world and the mental world are one and the same. Physical light pollution is like trash in your eyes; it obscures the vision. Trash in your head also obscures your vision just as effectively and probably more.

The propellers disturbed the natural phosphorescence in the water, and it lit up like a million fireflies trailing in the *Full Bloom's* wake. The head uses ocean water to flush, so at night without the lights on, the head sparkled too when flushed. Sparkling shit, it was special for those who bothered to look.

Thud. "Here." Darcy was handing drinks up to Bo.

"Thanks." Bo took both drinks so Darcy could climb the rest of the way up the ladder. She took the companion seat and put both feet up on the back rail.

"What's all that glittery stuff in the water?" she asked, staring into the wake.

"Fireflies taking a shit, millions of them."

"We used to catch them as kids in south Florida, over by the swamp," Darcy said. She never even questioned why they were in the water or why they were shitting or why Bo would know they were shitting.

"We would sell them for a penny apiece to some weird dude who said he sold them to a lab. I would always miss out on a dime 'cause I would put them on my nails and then smush the little suckers, and my fingertips would glow for an hour. It was cool. I was cool."

"That is cool, Darcy."

"Ya know, they don't blink after you smush 'em."

A red indicator on the plotter began blinking, and the instrument began beeping as well. Bo looked up, and it showed one half mile away from the target. He took a couple of big gulps from his drink and set it in the cup holder. His numbers were close, but he wanted to ease up on them and scout around with the bottom sounder to locate the exact spot. He cut *Full Bloom* back to trolling speed to examine the bottom. The sounder echoed hills that were sharp sloped and 600 to 800-feet high.

Bo knew about those hills, but he was looking for a place so deep it would be out of the sounder's range and would show only swirls of color coming up from the depths. The sounder sends a pulse down through the water and is reflected off of the bottom back to the boat. This echo is deciphered by the machine and displayed on the screen. Bo knew that the swirls he had seen and puzzled over before had to come from varying temperatures of water and not solid objects.

Fully focused and concentrating on the sounder screen, Bo searched in ever-widening circles. He concentrated and circled and unconsciously sipped his drink. He was in his own world, fishing, hunting, and had all but forgotten he was out there because of that stupid lure. Instinct had taken over. After four or five circles, he ran over the spot he had been looking for.

He reversed hard, stopping the boat dead, then slipped it into neutral. He waited thirty seconds for the sounder to catch up showing he was still over the underwater fire.

Darcy had been watching Bo watch the screen.

"Looks like the lava lamp I had in my room," Darcy said simply.

"Yeah. That's where fireflies come from. Right there," Bo told her, as he bounded down into the cockpit. Good ol' Bulldog was ready.

"Let her go, Bull."

The wire was so stiff on the reel that Bulldog had to help it along until about 100 feet had unspooled. Then it took off by itself, allowing the lighted lure to speed to the depths. Bo watched it in the gin clear water. He could still see it at 300 feet. It had cast an eerie glow under the whole boat. The boat seemed to be floating on a florescent cloud, as if it were about to be beamed up to the mother spacecraft.

"Cool," Darcy whispered loudly.

"This is kinda scary, Boss," Bulldog muttered suspiciously.

"Here, you hold it."

He handed the whole contraption to Bo. When Bo had figured 200 fathoms, he locked down on the reel, put the rod butt in the holder, and plugged in the electric motor.

Bo climbed the ladder back to the bridge and checked the sounder to see how far they had drifted. He was off the fire by 400 yards. In gear and at idle, Bo purposefully overshot the fiery target to allow for the drift time.

"It's a waiting game now, Darcy. You back me up with Atom. I tried. Ten roger?"

"What does that mean?"

"I mean you verify that I tried. I kept my promise. Ten roger?"

"Ten what?"

"Ten roger. That means okay in radio talk."

"I have never heard any deejay talk that friggin' way."

"Ten roger means okay. Okay?"

"Okay. Ten roger."

"Darcy, you've been here ... what, three or four days already, haven't you?" He settled into the captain's chair.

"I guess."

"You got any plans? Job? Goin' back? Crewing on another boat?"

"No."

"Do you have any money?"

"No."

"Well, I could spot you a ticket back to Lauderdale. How about that?"

"No."

"Do you have any idea what you're gonna do?"

"No."

Bo turned and checked the sounder. They had drifted off again. The diesels rumbled in idle as Bo headed back for the numbers. He did the same approach and overshot them, killed the engines, and all was silent.

"I'm gonna wait here and some rich guy will come along and take care of me," Darcy announced. Before Bo could respond, she added, "I'm gonna take care of him. I know how, too."

Bo just sat and sipped and listened to the waves slap the side of the boat.

"Boss! You see that fallin' star?" Bulldog yelled up to the bridge.

POW! CRACK! Zzzzzzzz! The rod exploded.

"Fish on!" Bo screamed involuntarily.

Something had hit so hard and with such sudden force that the rod cracked in half. The broken part tore into the water. Bulldog left the rod butt in the holder and hit the switch. The electric motor loaded up and gears ground. It was fish against machine. The machine was winning, but only slightly. A violin bow on that deep wire would have played the high notes and broken the safety glass on the cabin. The motor strained and strained. Bo was down in the cockpit getting an ice pack to cool it.

"What do you think it is?" Bulldog asked, hoping Bo would know.

"I have no idea."

Bo was holding ice all around the motor while the ice quickly returned to water. Everybody fixated down deep as the glow was slowly brightening.

About halfway up, at 600 feet, Bo said, "We gotta stop. This sucker's gonna melt. Maybe it'll hang on, whatever it is. We gotta chance it."

Bo filled the bag with ice again and went back to nursing the motor. Once the light escaped the surface of the water, it re-refracted a spooky neon that danced on all the white surfaces of the boat.

"You sure you don't know, Boss?"

"It's the mother of all fireflies."

"It's a big ass fly, Boss, a big ass fly for sure."

Bo hit the motor switch again. Gears ground and strained again. At 100 feet they could see the fish. They didn't know what it was, and it didn't really fight, but it was heavy as lead. At least it didn't have 20-foot long tentacles with suckers on them big as saucers. That made Bulldog feel much better.

"I can get him now, Boss," Bulldog said as he grabbed the gaff.

When the lighted lure broke the surface, only ten feet of leader was left until the hook and the fish. Bo took a wrap of the leader and pulled it close. Bulldog reached with the gaff while Bo held the wire.

"Nailed his butt!" Bo yelled as he stuck him solid, right under the gills. Bulldog turned the wire loose and helped his buddy slide the fish over the covering boards and slam onto the deck, dead.

"What the hell is *that*?" Bo said in disbelief. He raced up to the bridge to turn on the 2-million candle power halogen spotlights. These lights were so bright Darcy could have laid out in the fighting chair at night, worshipping under the sun god's night shift. Bo clambered back down, shook his head and went in for the rum. With the bottle by the neck he took a big swig and knelt down to examine this thing.

"Boss, I been on the water a long time and I done caught ever slimy thing that swims or shits in this here ocean, I figured, 'til now; but damn if I ever seen one of these rascals," Bulldog said in awe.

"It's pretty. What is it, Bo?" Darcy called from the bridge.

"It sure is a shiny ass fish. It looks like a saltwater catfish mated with a tarpon. I thought tarpon were pickier than this," Bo answered.

"There goes the neighborhood." Darcy had picked up on the mating problem.

The creature wasn't all that big, only five feet long, but for five feet it weighed more than any five-foot anything Bo had ever seen. This fish was pushing 180 pounds. It had the body of a catfish with a shovel snout and whiskers a foot and a half long. In fact, it might have just been a big saltwater catfish except it had huge scales like a tarpon, as big as silver dollars. Catfish don't have scales. Their skin is smooth as a baby's ass. These scales were silver bright in the halogen spotlights, almost platinum. Bo knelt down to examine its mouth.

"Gimme that big knife, Bull."

Bulldog handed him a banana blade knife, sharp as a razor and two feet long. Even though this thing looked and acted dead, Bo wanted a tool that maintained some distance. With the tip Bo pried the mouth open and peered inside. It looked normal, until Bo got to where the hook had set. Oozing from the gash made by the hook were yellow secretions.

"Holy shit!"

"What, Boss? What!" Bulldog went for his bat. The one thing he knew was with that bat he was a dragon slayer and to him this was a dragon, even if it was already dead. He was going to beat the shit out it anyway, just out of petrified principle. Just like anything humans are afraid of, when they kill it, they kill it. A snake isn't dead until it's in at least ten bloody pieces, with guts poring out, preferably.

"No, Bull. No!" Bulldog froze. Bo took the big banana knife and, whack, he sank that knife two inches into the middle of the thing's back.

"That's what I was fixin' to do, Boss."

"Just what I thought," Bo said as they silently watched yellow blood ooze onto the deck from the cut Bo had made.

"Yeah, just what I thought. Guys, it's only a yellow-blooded tarcat," Bo said. "Quite common, actually."

"Yeah, I've seen those ol' friggin' fish in Florida," Darcy added.

"Boss, I know you know damn near ever'thing. And, Boss, I know I don't know shit. But, Boss, I know you ain't never seen a fish like that 'cause I ain't never seen a fish like that. I bet it ain't even in the Bible 'cause I don't believe God even made that there fish."

"Bull, you're smarter than you think. I have never seen anything close. Darcy may have, but not me. Help me roll him over. Let's see what it eats and maybe that'll help us figure what this slime ball is all about."

Bo took the knife and slit it from gills to tail. Yellow and green chunks slid onto the deck. Bo couldn't make out what any of it was.

"What's that sack there? I ain't never seen that in a fish."

Bulldog was pointing to a grayish membrane sack the size of a softball, right behind and below the throat. Bo took the point of the knife and like a surgeon watched the tissue peel away like a wake behind a boat. The first cut revealed only more thickness. It was chicken gizzard tough. Bo went back for a second pass. That pass got through, and as it opened, a yellowish nugget clunked onto the deck. Bo picked it up and washed it in the cockpit sink. He held it up to the spotlights, and it radiated a soft yellow aura. Bo took the knife and gently tapped it. The tap left a mark. He put the nugget in his mouth and bit it. It was soft.

"I'll be a sonofabitch. This is gold," Bo whispered.

"Gold?" Bulldog said.

"Gold!" Darcy yelled.

"Gold," Bo repeated.

"GOLD!" they all screamed in unison.

Bo rifled through the tackle drawers and quickly found a four-ounce lead weight. In his left hand he held and juggled the lead weight. In his right hand he did the same with the nugget. Attempting to be a human balance, he declared, "Close to four ounces, if not over."

Darcy came down from the bridge. "I just want to hold it, pleeeese." Bo gave it to her.

"I like this now. I even like friggin' fishin'. Shit! I'm startin' to like you, Bo." Darcy was beyond excited.

"I wonder if there's any more," Bo said, as he reached for the knife.

"C'mon, Darcy, get a knife and dig in. Grub's up," Bulldog announced.

For the next thirty minutes, all that could be seen were their elbows and flashing knives feverishly mutilating that fish. Yellow blood splattered everywhere; green guts glistened and congealed in lumps. Gray membranes of organs were probed and fingered; purplish flesh and meat were sliced and diced. It was a horrific mess. Ghoulishness and grotesqueness go right over the side when it comes to greed and gold. When no part of that former fish was bigger than a quarter, Bo sat back and said, "I guess that's the only part that has gold."

"Shit, I was hopin' to find more," Darcy said.

"Me too, but four ounces a fish ain't bad," Bo said.

"Four ounces a fish ain't bad? Boss, you ever found any gold in *any* fish?" Bulldog put it in perspective, but the greed had already set in with Bo and Darcy. Gold rigor mortis.

They all rocked back on their haunches and laughed.

"We look like serial killers that did our whole serial in one shot," Bo said. "Where's that rum bottle?"

Bo looked around and found it. They passed the rum around as fish innards drooled off their hands onto the bottle, making it slippery and hard to hold.

"We got to clean this mess up before it dries," Bo said.

"Us, too," Darcy said as she began stripping off her clothes. Looking at the scene and circumstances, Bo began to strip too. What the hell? Bulldog joined in. As the clothes came off, they threw them all overboard. No way they would be clean again. Bo got the boat soap, sponges, scrub brushes, and the hose. They shared the cleaning supplies and lathered and scrubbed and lathered and, in between, took turns doing the same to the cockpit. It looked like one of those old-fashioned Saturday car washes school clubs put on to raise money.

When they and the boat were shined and polished, Bo went in to get towels and clothes. He returned with clothes Bulldog kept on the boat, and Darcy put on some of Bo's shorts and a T-shirt. Bo flung the old half bottle of rum overboard and went to get a fresh one; then he headed to the bridge. The big diesels rumbled to a start, and *Full Bloom* pointed to the hill.

Everybody was quiet, lost in their own thoughts. How much more is there? How many fish are there? What's my part? How much do I get? How much do I give them? What do I do with it? What now? Flip Flop.

———◆———

Full Bloom backed into a sleepy dock. It was 2 a.m., and just a few people passed by. A drunk who was kicked off a boat he couldn't score on went muttering by, while an older lady decided FiFi had to go whether FiFi wanted to or not. FiFi would fake it; Bo knew the type.

Once the boat was secured and plugged in, Bo called, "Bull, Darcy, come on inside." They all huddled around the table.

"Don't say a single damned word about tonight to anybody. Ten roger?"

"Ten roger." Bulldog nodded his head in agreement.

"Okay," Darcy agreed, too. "But what are we gonna do?"

"I don't know. I got to study and figure on this one a while. I've got to get a sample to Atom fast, to really check it out. Then if it's the real McCoy, we're gonna need more lures and all sorts of shit. I don't know ... I got to think. We do nothin' right now. Just don't say diddley squat to anybody!"

After Bulldog left, Darcy took Bo's hand. She knew and Bo knew this was inevitable, and the time had come. She led him below to the stateroom. Bo had been with other women and usually he was the aggressor. Man gets woman. This was different. He didn't want to be the aggressor. This girl had fascinated him from the moment she hit the dock. He wanted to see what she was all about.

She held him and pressed against him. Bo just stood there while she slowly undressed him. Each touch and brush of her hands sent warm shivers through his body. He tensed with anticipation. He laid back on the bed and she cupped all of him in her hands. She kissed him long and wet and with selfish purpose. Trailing her long blond hair across his chest, she moved her mouth down his body. Kisses, then licks, then all. She was murmuring as her head and mouth and tongue worked in ways Bo had never experienced. When his groin could take no more, she stopped. She knew. She smiled and he knew this girl wasn't stopping She was just beginning.

He glanced down and she was naked. She straddled him and guided him inside, working her hips as she deeply settled on him. She moved slowly, with intensity. She worked for herself. He opened his eyes and she was staring at him. Her whole body moved, her eyes locked on his eyes, steady and fixed and deter-mined. There was a hum inside her like a panther purring. Bo had never been more excited. He was mesmerized.

He pulled her closer and found those huge breasts with his mouth. She pushed harder and faster and the purr vibrated deep in both their bodies. Harder and faster and louder, then her buttocks squeezed so tight that she strained to hold on until Bo exploded. With her muscles, she milked.

She collapsed on him. His heart was pounding, and Bo could feel her heart pounding, too, right next to his. Their two hearts were talk-ing to each other in rhythm. When they had both caught their breaths, she rolled off and stretched long beside him. He was in another world. She kissed him on the cheek and whispered close in his ear.

"Round one! It's a draw." Wrapping her arms around him, she rolled him on top of her, spread her legs, grabbed his butt, laughed and said, "Round two, coming up."

Bo laughed back, a little nervously, "How many rounds is this bout?"

"Like anything in life, buddy Bo, ... 'til you can't get up."

CHAPTER 12

Bo woke right before first light. The stateroom lights had been dimmed to the lowest level and cast a warm, yellow glow. The same warm glow hung in Bo's heart, until he looked over at Darcy's naked body. She was barely covered, or uncovered, actually. The blanket lay only over one foot and half a leg. Her right hand rested on her left breast and was clutching something. The pose looked like a Emmy award. Very carefully, Bo uncurled her fingers and discovered the gold nugget. Bo thought, did she sleep with me or with the gold? He wondered, gold nuggets or my nuggets? The question worried him, but the answer worried him more.

Bo jumped into U-Boat. Triple clutching and nursing the transmission into second gear, he headed for the north end of the island, to Romero's house. Romero's sole purpose and goal in life was to swoon and proceed to mellowly molest the tourists, the good-looking female tourists.

Romero had ended up on Briland three years ago, through deception, and hadn't broken the habit. He had sinisterly schemed to marry a Bahamian girl in order to gain a Bahamian passport and escape his home country, Italy. Escape was a necessary part of the plan, then and now. On the same day Romero pledged his wedding vows in Nassau, his attorneys were pledging the sale of his drug store chain in Rome. The proceeds were immediately and directly wired to his account in the Bahamas, leaving the Italian government with its share of the deal somewhat lacking. The government's portion bought him a nice house on the ocean side that he named "Little Italy" out of reverent respect and abundant appreci-ation.

With much less respect, he left his bride in Nassau. As for the appreciation aspect of his marriage/citizenship, he told her that he needed time away to grow, so that he might gain *more* appreciation for her. However, absence was not making Romero's heart grow fonder. He was just stuffed full of respect and appreciation like an Italian sausage.

He had perfected his cunning craft to an art. Women would come down to the island seeking refuge and sun from the colder climes of Canada and Europe. They were in a romantic paradise thousands of miles away from husbands and boyfriends. He knew these women wondered, what's a harmless little fling to make this trip even more adventurous, daring and memorable? It was like the art of judo. Romero just pushed them in the direction they wanted to fall anyway. The arrangement served both parties. They got more than they came for and Romero, well ... he just came. Then they left for home; vacation over. Move your game piece to the next open space. Perfect. Flip Flop.

This cat and mouse game sometimes resulted in Romero's coughing up a pubic hairball. That had happened about a year ago. One morning Romero had driven in his golf cart the last night's catch to the beach, so she could sneak back unnoticed from her "early morning beach stroll." However, she happened to be there with a guy who had missed her and was up looking for the damsel. He caught the final kiss and the disembarkment. He couldn't chase both Romero and the girl, so he decided on Romero and started chasing him all over the island in his own golf cart.

It wasn't exactly Monaco at 12 miles per hour, but it definitely possessed the same intensity, and was as close to a hot car chase as these Briland natives were ever going to witness. They stood under the shade trees, on street corners, and on their porches cheering

Romero on, not wanting him to be caught, because a capture would end the festivities. Tires didn't squeal, but the gallery did. After several blocks, when Romero couldn't shake the boyfriend, he headed for the marina. Skidding to a stop on the boat ramp where Bo and Bulldog were throwing cast nets for bait, he bailed out.

"Bo! Bo! Youa gotta helpa me!" Romero came running, composure in shambles trailing behind him. The other guy was right on his heels.

"Hea crazy man!" Romero was pointing. The guy was huge. The island found out later he was a professional football player.

"I'm gonna kill that curly headed greaseball!" he shouted.

"Whoa! Whoa! Just wait a second," Bo said. "I know Romero here sometimes takes advantage of certain situations, but I have never known him to be less than a slick sorry ass gentleman. Always, consent on *both* sides, both sides mind you; that's part of the game. So I suggest you take this up with the other half, and I am sure the *better* half, before you lose it doin' something rash."

Bo had slowed the big guy a little with the speech, but it didn't stop him.

"If you're saying my little lady had anything to do with this shit, I'm gonna kill you too, you fish slime." He headed for both of them.

All of a sudden the whole crowd that had followed from their observation posts and gathered for the showdown began chanting, "Bulldog! Bulldog! Bulldog!" All eyes turned to follow.

Bulldog had picked up the guy's 600-pound golf cart and was carrying it over his head. He casually walked toward the edge of the water and, with the heave of a shot putter, Bulldog hurled that cart 30 feet into the bay. Bubble, bubble.

"You ought best lock the brakes on that thing when you get out, Mister," Bulldog said.

The guy stood frozen.

"Well, mister?"

Mr. Football turned and walked away, muttering and promising revenge. He and his girl took the afternoon plane out.

"Bo, Bo, Bo, my maina man. Ima owe you one. Ina my heart I will nota forget. *Capisce?*" Romero was shaking Bo's hand profusely.

"*Capisce*, Romero."

So now Bo was headed to Romero's to cash in the favor. Part of Romero's seduction arsenal included a high-powered, offshore racing boat. To most boaters, like Bo, it was good for nothing. If you couldn't fish off it, what good was it? In south Florida all the Romeros and wannabe Romeros had them. Bo and his buddies called them, "trip me, fuck me boats." Bo did find a need now. He had to get to Nassau and Atom fast.

"Romero! Romero!" Bo was rapping at the door. He waited.

"Romero! Get your ass up. Romero!"

"Bo! My maina man." Romero was slinking around the corner of the house with nothing but a towel wrapped around him. Bo should have known that there was no way Romero would come to the front door and show his face at that time of the morning.

"Romero, I need to get to Nassau, pronto. Like now."

"It's a Sunday."

"Like you're a man of the cloth. Sheets maybe. Let's go, *now*, Romero."

"Stepa around backa da house Bo. I gota business to finish, thena we go. Okay?"

"I don't have friggin' time for unfinished business, Romero."

"Oh, Bo, I done a finished. Justa say nice bye-bye, so shea come backa tonight. Capisce?" Romero went back inside while Bo nervously paced.

Through the screen door Bo heard, "Janice, Janet, uh, Janice."

"Joyce," a women's voice said.

"Ah yes, Joyce, my lovea, my lifea, my dearest one. Ia have to scoot away for a favor. Ia see you ona beach later, yes?"

"Yes, yes, Romero."

"Ah yes, my sweetness, ciao."

Bo was about to gag. "Get your ass out here!"

They jumped into U-Boat and crossed the Queen's Highway, which was one lane of dirt on this part of the island, and over to the bay side where Romero used a friend's dock to tie up his boat. Romero was wearing a tiny men's thong and a tank top. Bo wondered, who in the hell would even manufacture something like that, much less convince anybody to wear it? Romero needed to shave his legs and especially trim the crotch. It was disgusting. Bo found a beer in the ice box and chugged it to settle his stomach.

The 38-foot cigarette boat fired off with uncontrolled explosions. With no mufflers and straight pipes, it popped and cracked like repetitive rifle shots. Underlying, there was a serious rumble. These engines didn't like idle.

Romero gunned the monster engines and they stood with their butts backed against the padded baluster. They couldn't sit because they needed to flex their legs at the knees to absorb the shock. The boat left the water, came back down, bit again and was off. At 70 miles per hour on open ocean, it leapt from wave crest to wave crest, sometimes skipping one altogether and flying 100 yards through the air, before coming down again, for another bite of the water. It was a 110-decibel flying fish. At that rate Bo figured Nassau to be less than an hour away.

Indeed, fifty-two minutes later they were looking at Nassau. They avoided Nassau Harbour and went around the ocean side of Paradise Island at full bore. On the western side of New Providence Island, Bo guided Romero to help him weave through the coral heads toward the beach. Bo made Romero run the boat right up on the beach in front of the Cable Beach Hotel and Casino.

"Stay right here," Bo ordered. He knew he didn't have to tell Romero. There was no way Romero was going to try to re-negotiate the coral heads without him. Besides, there were girls on the beach. He jumped off and trudged through the thick sand toward the hotel. Bo contributed ten bucks to the desk clerk's future grand-children or a bottle of rum, whichever came first. In the Bahamas this really could be a serious contest. The clerk gave him Atom's room number and Bo rode the elevator to the eighth floor.

"Atom! Atom!" Bo said, rapping excitedly.

"What are *you* doing here?" Atom said surprised as he opened the door.

"You won't believe this," replied Bo. He held the nugget square to Atom's face. Atom backed away cross-eyed, trying to focus on that nugget in his face, like a vampire backs down from a cross. Bo told the whole story in such detail that Atom didn't need to ask for clarifications, and with such frantic speed he couldn't if he had wanted to.

"I told you. Did I not tell you? Did I not tell you there would exist some curious life forms down there we have never explored to date, or observed before? We just never attempted the search until now. Refraction reaction!" Atom was as excited as Bo.

"What do we do now?"

"Firstly, we have to make sure. Verify this sample truly is gold."

"It's gold; I know *gold*. Remember when I came to Tech visiting you and I panned for it every time I could go up to Dahlonaga?"

"Bo, I'm a scientist. I like to be sure. I never guess. What do you want to do? Take it to a jeweler on Bay Street and pawn it? Your impatience would smash the atom before it was even in the accelerator."

"Whatever that means - you're probably right. Well?"

"I'll preside over the morning presentation and hand this after-noon's session off to my co-chair. I'll catch the first afternoon flight back to Atlanta. The metallurgy lab is headed by a good friend of mine and he owes me a couple of big favors. I will call him and give him a heads up. By the morning we'll know exactly what we've really got here."

"Ten roger, buddy, but what after that?"

"I don't know yet; one step at a time. Oh, the velocity of time! It's almost 0900. I've got to go. I will call you in the morning. Take two aspirin with a quart of rum." They rode the elevator down together in silence, the way most elevator riders do. However, their silence was for other reasons; they were both sheer dumbstruck at the prospects.

Bo walked out to the beach, looking down at the sand, and muttered, "Please, please, please."

Romero had four beach bunnies in the boat with the stereo cranked to max playing some Bob Marley.

"All right, you little bunnies. Scram!"

"Bo, Bo, don't talka to the ladies with sucha tones."

"Sorry. Get the hell off the boat."

"Ladies, ladies, he not Italiano lover likea me. I be backa soon. Funna in the sunna. Ciao! " Romero kept chattering as he tossed beers to them like consolation prizes.

They shoved the rocket off the beach, fired it up, and Romero was flashing his best seducing smile and waving as they motored out through the coral. "Trip me, fuck me boats," Bo thought, for sure. It was just about 10 o'clock when they tied to the dock on Briland. Bo dropped Romero back at his house.

"Thanks, Romero. I really do appreciate it."

"Favor for favor, the Italian way. Bo, try to loosen up likea me. Bea lover, Bo."

"See ya around. Tight lines to ya, Romero." Bo rambled south on down the Queen's Highway.

CHAPTER 13

While U-Boat's engine was chucking and checking, Bo's mind was calculating. Now he needed money more than ever. More than yesterday, more than all the yesterdays. He had to rebuild that engine or maybe both while he was at it. Now he really had to depend on his boat. He needed lights, lures, several big electric reels, heavy back-boned rods, miles of wire, and a shitload of other stuff. It was like setting up a business from start. Then it hit him, and he hit the brakes. He realized, that for once in his life, his money problems could be over.

Just then a mangy dog ambled across the sand road with tits hanging so low they dragged on the ground. She needed food to make food. Bo whistled and the dog sidled up sideways like a crab walks, with her nipples leaving signature lines in the sand. Bo reached under the back seat for a loaf of stale bread he used to crumble on the water to attract bait fish. The dog stood there with bleary weeping eyes, hoping.

"Bitch, this is my lucky day and I'm gonna make it your lucky day, too. All you got to do is stand there a few minutes and listen to my ass and this loaf of bread is yours. Ten roger?

"I am a charter captain and a fisherman and a damn good one. That was all I ever wanted, and I got just what I wanted. You always get what you want, if you want it bad enough. God programmed hormones in you to want to screw for a whole week and that's what you wanted, real bad. You got what you wanted. Then after all these years, *you* change. You change, not charter fishing, it's the same, but *you* change. You changed too, bitch. Look at your sorry ass. You get what you want, then you want more. In six months you'll want more again. You won't learn, and we don't either."

The dog started to move.

"Here." Bo threw a couple of slices. "I guess you've earned that much so far."

Bo expected the dog to practically inhale the bread without chewing, but she was so weak that she labored with one slice at a time.

"I don't fish anymore. I'm a hired servant. I'm day labor, a high priced hooker. Hooking people, not fish. They come on my boat, my home, obnoxious, drunk, and loud. They spill shit everywhere, puke all over, use the towel rack in the head as a hand hold, and in rough seas rip it out of the wall. When it goes, they go all over the floor and laugh. They have a big-deal-we-paid-for-it attitude. Then they bring their whores over here from Lauderdale and want to use my bed to fuck the trash in and say, 'we bought the whole boat didn't we?' I've been no better then the whores they shipped in from Lauderdale and probably worse than the whores they shipped back out. They dribble their sorry little wads on them after their macho calisthenics and then piss beer buckets on my deck, walking out laughing, 'we paid for it,' what's the friggin' difference? What's the friggin' difference, dog, ten roger?"

He threw a couple more slices.

"No mas, mon, no more. Zippo, zero, sayonara to all that shit. This is my lucky day, and yours too. I will never hire my boat, my home, or me out again. I declare, and as you are my esteemed witness, bitch, I am from this day forward, *not* a charter captain any more. I am NOT for hire. I am now a gold prospector and I'm gonna find a shit pile of it. I'm in the gold business now, bitch, and you know what? You're in the bread business now. Gold is my bread and bread for you is, well, just bread; no offense, it's all relative.

I didn't learn. I lucked up. You're not gonna learn either. You lucked up. Today, now, this very moment. Since you can't learn, after you get those puppies up and run off, I'm gonna get you fixed. Dog, I'm fixin' to get fixed, too."

Bo threw the whole bag of bread. The dog snatched up the corner and dragged it and her tits through the brush to her litter. Bo cranked U-Boat and ground it into gear. Heading back down the Queen's Highway of sand, he yelled back, "Hey, bitch, I'll see you tomorrow!" He meant it, too.

CHAPTER 14

A sleek Gulfstream IV private jet cruised overhead with landing gear hanging and setting up the approach to North Eleuthera airport. Ward's back, Bo said to himself, and then another flash hit him. Ward would help him and not ask questions. Ward was an extremely wealthy man, and he was a good man, too. On occasion he had offered to lend Bo money, and had pretty much left the matter an open door. Bo had never taken him up on the offers partly out of pride, but mostly because he was never quite sure how he could repay the loan. He valued Ward's friendship more than a way to get out of his constant financial jams.

But it was different this time, he thought. Now he was sure he could repay any loan and in record time as well. He would see him later down on the dock because Ward and his wife's boat, *ForWARD*, was coming in. *ForWARD* was an extravagant floating palace; it was 150 feet long and supported by a crew of eight. Instead of floating the usual champagne and caviar parties, the boat had lately become something of a freight barge, ferrying tons of support and supplies for their daughter's upcoming wedding, dubbed around the island, the "Royal Wedding." Honey's wedding had been planned for a year and she wanted the festivities on Briland and on the beach. Bo liked them even more for choosing the island since they could have done it anywhere in the world.

The story goes that Blanche, Honey's mother, called a French gentleman to inquire about renting his house. The beautiful house was graced with enormous royal palms and was right on the beach. Honey, or maybe Blanche, had chosen that house for the wedding setting. The Frenchman flatly told Blanche he would not rent the house. Blanch then asked about buying it and was even further rebuked by the Frenchman.

"How about $4 million?" she offered simply with a warm smile. Sold. They were not to be denied.

They then proceeded to build pools and pool houses, to dredge the bay side for ForWARD, to completely redo the main house, and generally pour another $3 million into the place. Blanche had told Bo one time she bought the house so her kids would have a place to go. What astonished Bo was, when she said it, she wasn't boasting or joking. She sincerely meant it, just that way. Everything is relative, Bo thought. Ward had everything; he wasn't worried. Ulmer had nothing; he wasn't worried. Bo figured it must be the masses in between that shouldered the world's worries. He would run into Ward this afternoon.

Back in town, Bo spotted Ulmer kicked back in his strapless lawn chair, plying his trade.

"Uncle Ulmer! What's up, mon?"

"Cap Bo! Wanna beer?"

"No, thanks, too much to do."

"How bout dis?" Ulmer revealed the water-stained piece of plywood he was drawing on with the reverence of a master sharing a private, privileged peek at his latest work, kind of a sneak preview. Bo scanned it quickly. It was something about "my tummy sticks out farther than my dickie do."

"It's a little deep."

"They figgur; no problem, mon."

"Ulmer, I'm about to hit big. I mean big time, man."

"You head come roun' and you 'cided to be my agent, huh?"

"Only you could sell this stuff, Ulmer. No, I've discovered something, but I can't tell you what yet."

"Bo, you needs to scover you self fuss. Den you kin scover all you lil' heart's desire. You self fuss, Bo; scover you self fuss."

"I know, Ulmer, but that's hard, and this came along first any-way. After this discovery, I can buy a new self every month. Not only that, man, but I can buy a new boat every month, and a new friggin' chick to go along with each one of them."

"Don't count dose chicks befo day hatches. Fact, don't even count dose eggs befo day drop, even gold eggs, Bo."

"Why did you say gold?"

Uncle Ulmer just smiled and the gold fillings in his teeth shone.

"Why did you say gold, Ulmer?"

The smile got broader.

"That smart ass island voodoo. I got to go. Tight lines to ya."

"Be good, Bo." Ulmer got back to his proverbs. Bo headed back to the dock.

Bulldog was in the cockpit straightening up tackle and just gen-erally piddling. Darcy was stretched out on the foredeck bench, sacrificing her body to the sun gods.

"Where you been, Boss?"

"I went to Nassau to give the gold to Atom. I want him to take it back and analyze it for real. We'll know tomorrow."

"I know now, Boss. Cain't be nothing but gold comin' out of a fish like that. That's the damnedest fish I ever seen. You know what, Boss? We still don't know what it eats. We need to find out if we plan to grab some more of em'. Squid, or ... maybe it was just luck, Boss."

Bulldog was right. And, Bo thought, this guy *has* got a logical mind. Bo had seen it before, real logic. Bulldog's only problem was most of the time he operated in the heart mode, not the mind mode. That sometimes got Bulldog in trouble, but it was always trouble that worked out for the good in the long run. Bo, on the other hand, operated solely in mind mode, and he stayed in trouble, too. The big difference was, his plan almost *never* worked out for the best. The thought caused Bo to pause, but not long enough.

"Bull, we need wire, reels, tackle, Atom's lures, not to mention engine work, generator work, *man*, a shit pile of stuff."

"I know. I been thinking, Boss. We need trolling valves on the transmissions to slow this thing down and stay on top of 'em. We sure as hell ain't gonna anchor in 3,000 feet of water. And drag chutes, well, I thought about that, too, and they gonna drift too fast."

Bo had never even thought about those problems. Bulldog not only had, but he'd also figured out the answers.

"I'm impressed, Bull. You've done some hard studying. What's got into you?"

"Boss, I need whatever little share of that gold you gonna give me. I reckon there's enough that even just a smidgen could buy Christmas for every kid on this island. I dreamed last night maybe Christmas for all of 'em over on Eleuthera, too. I know it's just a dream, but maybe, Boss, ... just maybe."

Bulldog's eyes were leveled at Bo and the fat of his brow kept them down and the fat of his cheeks held them up, keeping them locked, fat locked, steady and determined. Bo had to look away, look into the water, look anywhere. His mind had been consumed with bigger boats and a better class of bimbos. In Bulldog's presence now, he felt ashamed. He knew he should think more about giving, but shit, he hadn't got *his* yet. Well, he thought, Bulldog's so good, his giving will just balance it out. That's it.

"We'll get 'em, Bull. Let's get to work."

Bo looked down the dock at *ForWARD* and thought he saw Ward on the back deck headed inside. He figured, now is as good a time as ever. *ForWARD's* Captain John was just coming off the gangway when Bo walked up.

"Hey, John, how's it going?"

"Good, Bo, how's fishing?"

"Just a couple of blues since you were here last, but there's a lot of dolphin and tuna. Y'all goin' out?"

"I think Ward wants to. He's real pissed off with his new fishing boat, though. He's anxious to break the jinx or find out what's wrong. I counted up 150 hours of trolling without a marlin strike. That's unheard of. Ward swears it's the props, but I think the rudders rattle, scaring them off."

"Its some weird stuff, I agree. Did I see Ward onboard?"

"Yeah, he's somewhere."

"You know if he's busy?"

"I don't think so. I'll go find him. Come on board."

Bo dropped his shoes at the door and entered money. The foyer floor was marble from Italy that ran into a wall of cream-colored suede from Argentina, which had a shadow cast on it by a gold pedestal topped with an Oriental Ming dynasty vase displaying three dozen fresh, yellow roses. All lighting was indirect from sources tucked in valances, except for the pinpoints of light coming from the smoke gray-blue mirrored ceiling. The carefully designed effect created the appearance of twinkling stars on a beautiful night.

To the left was a huge open salon filled with chairs and sofas soft as down. There were dozens of throw pillows of all colors, deep, but muted and framed in real gold braided piping. Also in the salon was a bar made of carrera marble, glass, and even more gold. Bo knew it was well stocked, but the bottles were stowed below so it had that real clean look. There were four bar stools, and it was reported the seats were covered in whale foreskin. Bo wondered how many times some tipsy guest had infuriated some prim ass socialite by announcing, "Hey, lady, you know you're sitting on a whale dick?"

Ward came around the corner.

"Hey, Bo, how have you been?" Ward greeted him genuinely, holding out his hand.

"I'm fine, Ward. How about you? Blanche and the kids?"

"Everybody's great, but this wedding is getting crazy. It's damn near a movie production. Just because of the logistics of transferring that many people here, I'm having to use friends' jets, as well as charter. The house and pool house are coming along on Bahamian time, which as you know, means infinity. Planning a sit-down dinner for 300 guests when there aren't 300 chairs, including Ulmer's lawn chair, on the whole damn island, isn't exactly fun either."

"Blanche will pull it off. Y'all going out?"

"Yeah, I've got to find out what's up with my fishing boat. I've never seen anything like it, and neither has anybody else. This will be the fourth set of props I've tried. If this doesn't work, I'm just going to sink it. Why don't you go with us and see what you think?"

"I'd like to help, Ward, but I'm in the middle of a big project, which is why I need to talk to you. I need a loan. Just short term, but with obscene interest."

"You know I'll always help you, Bo. How much?"

"Twenty-five grand."

"No problem. All I ask, is this project legal?"

"Absolutely, but one day when I tell you, it will look like stealing."

Ward went around to the bar, opened a drawer and pulled out a faded blue, vinyl plastic checkbook, standard issue from the bank, and started writing. Bo thought that checkbook looked just like his, but that was where the similarity stopped dead.

"Here you go, Bo."

"Ward, I really appreciate it. I won't let you down. By the way, I think your boat problem is the transmissions. They whine a certain frequency that's running everything in the ocean off. It's like fingernails on a blackboard. Have John drain half the fluid and I'll give him a special formula to replace it. You'll catch the big momma."

"That boat cost me a half a million dollars. If what you say is true and your formula works, you won't owe me a dime."

"It'll work, and I will still owe you. Count on both. I gotta run.

Thanks again, Ward. Tight lines to ya."

"Listen up on the radio. I'll call you if we hook up. Hell, I'll call and announce it to the whole damn world on the satellite system."

Bo and Bulldog sat huddled over all the fishing gear catalogs on the boat. They were stacked several feet high and they catalog shopped until they had to stand up. With three legal size pages full, Bo headed to the bridge to call in the orders on the single-side band, an extremely strong radio that could call up the high seas operator located in Miami.

"W.O.M., W.O.M., this is the *Full Bloom*, whiskey sierra delta, six, four, seven, seven."

The radio operator answered and requested a location in order to tune his antennas for peak performance. Once maximum reliable contact was established, Bo requested a land operator. This was an expensive way to communicate, but sometimes it was all there was in the Out Islands to link them to the rest of the world. The island's phones were out again. Bo was calling in the first order to the supply house, when he suddenly remembered that anyone on the ocean could hear the conversation. He couldn't be ordering all this gear and telling the world about it. He quickly terminated the call.

Bo decided he would give his order list to some pilots he knew who flew the route every day, to and from the states. They would give the list to his tackle buddy, Roy, in Lauderdale to manage the purchases. Funding in place and ordering started, he was in business.

It was that time of day when the sun signaled drink time. Bo made a whopper for himself and one for the freshly showered Darcy. They sat on the bridge listening to Jimmy Buffett and sipped silently together, but far apart.

"What now, Bo?"

"I don't know. That is, I don't know yet."

"I know we got gold."

"What's this 'we' shit? I got gold."

"Look, asshole, I may not have helped, but I was there, and I know about it. We are supposed to keep it a secret, right? Or ten roger, or whatever the fuck you say ?"

Bo picked up on the extortion immediately and said nothing.

"Cut me in, and then you can cut me out."

"Ten roger, but I was hoping for more than ..." he trailed off like a dying generator. Generators just quietly run down, quit, and then cost you a lot of money.

"I got some new flip-flops, see?" She held them up with the price tag dangling.

Damn if they weren't on the wrong feet. The tag fluttered like a Jolly Roger pennant signaling "Warning, Danger." For some reason the conversation was as awkward as the flip-flops.

"I've got to go to bed. It's been a long day, Darcy. Will you come?"

"Naw, I'm getting a second wind. I'll go talk to Sandy and hang out at the bar awhile."

Bo headed down the ladder, with Darcy following. He went in, and she went out. No words. They were both too uncertain and too confused to talk, not to just each other but even to their own inner bearings. Bo eased into bed and thought of *The Old Man and the Sea*. Darcy went to the bar.

CHAPTER 15

Raindrops splattered on his head. Bo woke to an open hatch but, as always, an open outlook for the new day. Darcy lay quietly beside him, and he was grateful. He didn't bother her. He wanted to, but he was a man on a mission and the mission had just begun. She could wait, or maybe he couldn't wait. Priorities.

With the order list tucked in his back pocket, he jumped into *The Bud* and steered toward Three Island Dock to meet his pilot buddies.

"Jeff!" Bo yelled against the noise of the plane's engines.

"Bo, how you doin'? I've got a fax for you. It came just as we were leaving."

"Trade you. I've got a letter for you to give to Roy at Bluewater Tackle."

They traded carefully, the prop wash whipping the correspondence. Bo sat at the picnic table outside the 'Dis an 'Dat Shop across from the airport. The plane took off to Governor's Harbour as Bo first peeled, then impatiently tore, the envelope open.

Bo,
It *is* GOLD. Gold as pure as any sample the guys have ever seen. Will assemble two dozen more lures ASAP. Should have them to you by next week. I told you, buddy. Didn't I tell you!?"
Atom
Note: Try bait other than just squid; that could have been just luck.

Bo sat. The note part sounded just like what Bulldog had said; they think alike. He had known it was gold, but the confirmation was like a batter hitting the ball, knowing it was going over the fence, yet running slowly and watching until it actually fell in the stands. Until it fell, your heart just didn't know. It fell now, all right, like a brick, a *gold* brick. He and that mangy lil draggin' dog were fixin' to make it big. He bought two loaves of *fresh* Bahamian bread.

Later in the afternoon, Bo did use the single-side band to call his mechanics in Lauderdale and reported all the problems with both engines and the generator. They were to bring every part they might need, but no more, since duty to the Bahamian government would be due on all imported parts. He then checked with Bluewater to see if they had gotten the list.

"What the hell are you doin', Bo?" Roy at Bluewater asked, like Bo was out of his mind.

"It's an experiment, Roy. Let's not talk about it on the radio."

"Are these numbers right; ten mega-electric, wire line rigs?"

"Yeah, ten. Now hush."

"Okay. I'll have to send someone to Miami. I'm short some of this stuff."

"Roy. Fast. Pronto. You got it? Money is no object."

"Whatever, Bo. Let me get to work."

"I've got mechanics coming over on a chartered 9 o'clock tomorrow. Meet them at Executive Airport, Banyan, and put all the gear you can find on the plane."

"I can get most of it by then, Bo, but it'll cost you."

"Give me the clergyman's price, Roy."

"Ten roger, but you ain't no clergyman, Bo."

"Tight lines to ya, buddy. AT&T High Seas, this is *Full Bloom*. We're finished. You can give me back to W.O.M., thank you."

"*Full Bloom*, High Seas, are you done?'

"Yes, thank you."

"Have a good watch. High Seas out."

"*Full Bloom*, W.O.M."

"This is *Full Bloom*. We're done. Thank you."

"Have a good watch. Any other traffic on this channel?"

Silence.

"No traffic. W.O.M. out."

There was someone on that channel, but he didn't speak. It was the owner of the color-matched Post Bo had cursed and admired directly across the dock from him.

"Do you know any other boats named *Full Bloom*?" he asked the mate.

"No, sir. *Full Bloom*, right there behind us, is a pretty well known sportfishing boat in these parts; at least the captain is. He's one of the best."

"He's up to some shit. We use our electric reels only a couple of times a year. Why in the hell would somebody want ten, and the biggest ball-busters they make at that?"

"Beats me."

"Find out."

"That'll be easy. He's got some real dumb boat bimbo on the boat. She'll talk and not even know she's talking. Mighty fine looking bimbo at that."

The next few days were as frantic as Bo could make them. The mechanics were up to their elbows in grease, tearing both engines down to rebuild them. Roy had come through with just about all Bo had ordered. Bulldog bent to the task of rigging rigs, sharpening hooks, winding and twisting wire.

Even Darcy got out of the sun and into helping. Bo couldn't believe it. She had no problem jumping into the engine room and handing the mechanics tools, rags, and ice water; just generally tending to them. Bo reasoned, she figured the only way she could help was to do the only thing she knew how to do, which was to "serve." They had never had a helper like Darcy. "Boss Bimbo" they called her, good-naturedly. She didn't care, her glowing skin was thick, too. They just worked their asses off to impress her with their mechanical manliness.

Bo directed the work, nervous as a June bug in a chicken coop. When Bo wasn't watching over everybody else, his job was to install new battery banks and electrically rewire the whole cockpit to power the new electric arsenal. In Bo's mind, this was war and preparations were underway for the invasion.

"We're gonna slaughter the bastards," Bo told Bulldog.

"Yeah, if we don't sink the boat with all this gear first."

"This boat's hauled your fat ass around for years. It'll take it."

"Boss, if you cain't fish with the big dogs, stay at the dock."

"That's the spirit, Bull. That's the spirit."

CHAPTER 16

After three 20-hour days, the onslaught was almost finished. They were all so tired every night that a hot shower and a cold drink put them out. Bo was too tired to have sex with Darcy, despite her attempts, even when she got on top so he wouldn't have to work at it. Every evening before bed, Bo had been making excuses about running out to "finish up a few things."

That evening while they were on the bridge with an ice cold rum bottle, Darcy turned to Bo and jokingly said, "Bo buddy, I *think* you've got some whore you're visiting every night before bed."

"How in the world do you think my worn-out ass could do that?"

"Worn-out ass is right. Who's wearing you out? You won't even touch me."

"Darcy, Darcy, Darcy. Come on, I'll show you where I been goin'."

They jumped in U-Boat and headed north up the Queen's Highway. Almost at the end of the end of the north end, Bo stopped and whistled. Out of the thick brush crawled the dog, looking better, but still pretty dilapidated. Darcy jumped out and ran for the dog.

"Oh, Bo! Look. This poor dog needs help."

Bo grabbed a loaf from under the seat.

"Here, gimme that." Darcy was coming for the bread.

"Here, poor baby. Poor baby. Look at her, Bo. Here, momma, here's some bread." She started feeding one slice at a time. "I'm a professional server you know and I'm gonna serve you with the best service I know. Poor baby."

"Damn, Darcy, you're talking to a dog. You act like that mangy mongrel knows what you're talking about."

"She understands. Don't you, baby?" Darcy cooed, making soothing sounds to the dog while she fed her. Bo sat silently in U-Boat's worn canvas seat, sipping rum and looking at the stars. When the dog had gummed through the last slice, Darcy stood up.

"OK, momma, I'll take care of you from now on. You run back to your puppies and take care of them. See you later, baby." The dog skittered sideways into the brush.

"Poor thing. All right, let's go. Where in the hell are we going anyhow?"

"This is where I come every night," Bo said simply. "I've been feeding that sorry bitch."

"Oh! No! Not you? Not *you*, Mr. Mission Man. Mr. Cold Heart."

"Yeah, me."

They both went silent. Hard ass Bo, and bad ass Darcy. U-Boat rumbled back down the sand road. That night Bo and Darcy made love and didn't have sex. Flip Flop.

CHAPTER 17

The time had finally come. *Full Bloom's* crew prepared to set out after the secret gold. The cockpit had been rewired, the mega-wire lines rigged, the engines rebuilt, and trolling valves installed. Chris came racing down the dock in his new Nike shoes, which were, at his age of eleven, his total identity.

"Cap'n Bo. Cap'n Bo. Da customs man want you ova at da guvment dock."

"Got to be the lures. Let's go. Oh, we can't let anybody see those lures. Bull, I want you to use all the bulk you have to shield those lures from anybody seeing 'em. Darcy, anybody that gets around Bull, you distract them any way you can. I mean *any* way. Ten roger?"

"Ten roger, Boss."

"Okay, Boss ass."

Everything in the Bahamas comes in by boat. Nothing is built or manufactured there. All food, clothes, building materials, fuel, transportation, everything comes from somewhere else. It all arrives by small freighters plying the waters to the islands. As a consequence, the government has built substantial docks on each island to support the trade. On every island of any real population, just like the Queen's Highway and Bonefish Joe, every island's got its own Government Dock. The dock served both as the island's window to the world, and the center of the island's own little world.

The Bahamas have no income tax, property tax, or sales tax. The total revenue in the islands is collected through duties on incoming goods. The duty scale ranges from a low ten percent on living necessities, like food and clothes, to 100 percent on luxury items like a Mercedes Benz. All in all, however, it's a pretty fair and equitable system. As a result of this system, the customs man is a very powerful fellow. He has the authority to establish a price on anything. By virtue of what he thinks something is worth, he can cost you money. That's powerful. The wisdom of the Bahamian government is to move these customs guys around so they wouldn't have time to get too chummy with the locals and begin giving breaks to buddies.

"Mr. Cooper. How are you?" Bo greeted the customs man as casually as he could. Bo wanted no problems and no attention.

"Hi, Cap'n Bo. What's in dis box?" Mr. Cooper asked in the same tone of voice all government workers in every country use. There has got to be an international school that teaches them all how to talk with detached authority, threats, and impatience. They teach it by the book, learn it by the book, and love dispensing it by the book. They really, in Bo's mind, hide behind the book.

"Why, I don't know. Let's see who it's from. Atlanta. Georgia Tech."

"Open it."

Bo unsheathed his fishing knife from his belt and sliced the tape. Packing popcorn fluttered about the dock in the breeze. Bo reached in and felt the round plastic. He wiggled it out, trying to keep the popcorn in, and produced the lure. He held it low and casually as Bulldog jogged back and forth like a pro football guard keeping the curious onlookers from seeing it.

"What is it?" Mr. Cooper asked.

"It's a new engine part to get greater fuel efficiency."

The crowd was milling back and forth, too, some even on tip-toes. Bulldog was having a hard time.

"Let me see it." Mr. Cooper took it from Bo, and held it high, like he could see it better if it was higher. He held it by the tips on the ends and when he did, the moisture in his hands kicked it on. It glowed. Wow, what the shit, and jeezuzs murmured through the crowd.

"Now what is it really, Bo? What you hiding?"

"All night long, uh-huh ... all night long ... ," blasted from the speakers in U-Boat as everybody's heads turned to see Darcy. There she was in all her glory, topless, standing up in the back of U-Boat, making love to the roll bar like a stripper in Lauderdale.

The wow, what the shit and jeezuzs ratcheted up several notches. Moms were hiding children under their big, loose skirts trying to shield them, while the guys began migrating toward the jeep in a kind of celestial pull. Gravity rules, but Darcy wasn't letting gravity have anything to do with her body. Mr. Cooper also headed for the U-Boat. He didn't have taxes in mind. Pandemonium broke out with half the crowd running away from the scene and the other half running toward it.

"Woman! Get down from there! Woman! Put your clothes on! Stop! Stop that right now! Woman!"

"Grab the box, Bull, and get your ass outta here!" instructed Bo. With the box in front of him, Bulldog's mass covered it. He rolled on. Bo ran to the jeep.

"Darcy! Stop! Stop! Oh, Mr. Cooper, I'm so sorry. She's had another attack. Exhibitionitis. Real rare."

"What?"

"Exhibition-tits. I mean exhibition*itis*. Her medicine is on the boat. I've got to get her back for the shots, fast." Bo threw a plastic slicker over her entire body. He wrestled her from the roll bar and whispered to her, "good girl." Acting as if she was having a fit, Bo managed to get her into the seat and she sat huddled under the plastic, shaking uncontrollably. To the crowd, the shaking was the aftermath of either a fit or voodoo. Darcy was laughing her ass off under the slicker. Bo cranked U-Boat.

"I've got to get her medicine real quick!"

"Bo, you come over to da office at da airport fuss ting 'morrow, you hear?"

"Yes sir, Mr. Cooper."

Bo threaded U-boat through the crowd and off the dock with the girl under the slicker still shaking and leaving the crowd shaking too, but just their heads.

CHAPTER 18

At 11 o'clock that night Bo eased *Full Bloom* from her slip. Darcy took her usual place by him in the companion chair, feet propped up on the rail, while Bulldog was readying the tackle. The lures were nestled in the charging rack, sucking up electricity and getting ready for battle and riches.

An hour later, they were on the numbers, the water below began to show color on the depth sounder; first the lower deep purples, then bright reds, followed by the oranges, and turning into yellows that swirled, curled, and danced like a camp fire. Bo backed the throttles off and went below to turn on the new trolling valves. Back on the bridge and excited about this new venture, Bo shouted to Bulldog, "Let two fly, Bull."

"Aye, aye, Boss."

The wire peeled off the huge reels, just singing.

"Two more, Bull."

The four reels were singing so close in frequency to each other, they created an eerie pulsing harmonic. With four lures in the water, *Full Bloom* floated on clear, light green neon. The boat could have been a spaceship looking for a landing. The souls on board had no idea where they wanted to land, except Bulldog. He knew.

"Wow! This is some neat shit, Bo," Darcy whispered.

"Just tryin' to stay on top of the food chain, baby doll. Stayin' on top of the food chain, that's all we can do. Hell, that's the best we can do and we're mighty little in this big ass ocean. Maybe it would be easier in a smaller pond; then we would be bigger or just think we're bigger. But I like the big pond, the Mother Ocean."

Bo cruised *Full Bloom*, in very slow one-knot circles, around the underwater steam vents nature had created. Nobody said anything; each was absorbed in their own thoughts and wonder about the future of this craziness. There was silence, except for the constant rumble of the engines and the occasional slap of the water on the hull. Thirty minutes went by.

"It's night. I'm getting a drink," Bo announced. He swung down from the bridge, and as soon as his feet hit the cockpit deck, one of the monster reels screamed. Zzzzzzzz!

"Fish on!" Bulldog hollered. Bo grabbed the cockpit control and snatched the boat into neutral. Bulldog was all over the reel, cranking down on the drag and trying to turn the fish around. The new wire still peeled, silver under the lights and zig-zagging back and forth as it came off the spool.

"Get his gold ass, Bo! Get him, Bo! Get him, Bo! Get his gold ass! I need it! I need it baaad!" Darcy was yelling from the bridge. Bo and Bulldog were both holding the rod, trying to relieve some of the pressure on the rod holder.

"Get your ass down here and get him, Darlin', if you think you can do this any better."

"I'll get him, Bo. You wait. Just hang on to that rod like you would your dick, buddy."

The reel was still screaming, but slowing. Bo and Bulldog were straining. Darcy was yelling, "Get him, Bo! Get him! Get him! Get his gold ass!"

Three hundred yards of wire had come off the big reel before the spool turned no more. Bo hit the switch, and the electric motor clunked into the gear box and reversed the spool to harvest the wire.

"Bull, hit the switches on the other three. We need to get them in so they won't be in the way. Watch 'em close. These big motors will rip the tips right off these rods if you cut back too late.

"Ten roger, Boss."

The gear motor and reel strained, but was steady as it recovered wire. As the wire built up and piled onto the spool, the diameter of the spool got bigger, making the drag setting more effective. Bo dialed back off the drag, little by little, to compensate for the increase; otherwise, the fish could try to run again and snap even this wire. Atom had explained the mechanical dynamics of all that to Bo years ago. Bo didn't understand it then or now. Atom knew because he understood. Bo knew because he just knew. Bo was good. It came naturally. He was the best in the business.

Everybody grew quiet. Straining to get the first glimpse, three pair of eyes followed the wire into the clear, green water. Excited, nervous anticipation. Their minds had been in three far-flung directions 30 minutes before, but they were all in sync now. Is it another one? Please let it be. What if it is? What if it isn't? What now?

Darcy saw it first because she was higher up on the bridge.

"Hot shit! It's a gold fish, y'all!"

"Really?" Bulldog yelled.

"Really, Bull! I'd lie to Bo buddy, but I wouldn't ever shit you, Bull. Fuckin' A."

The wire kept coming, and Bo had him up to the leader now. This one was bigger than the other one.

"I figure this one will top two-fifty," Bo guessed as he worked the rod around.

"Get the gaff, Bull. I'll wire him right to the swim platform."

The big fish was dead or close to it. He was on his side, not moving at all. The gill plates were puffed open like he died trying to get that last rush of water, but it just wasn't enough. The scales of the fish glittered and sparkled in the florescent-lit water, shooting laser beams of light through the depths. It was a fitting sight for what lay inside this beast.

"He still might be alive, Bull, so stick him deep, right in the heart. Ten roger?"

"Ten roger, boss."

Bo guided the bulk to the stern of the boat.

"Now! Stick him!"

Bulldog snatched back, smart and quick. The razor gaff dug deep into the belly. The fish doubled up sideways in slow motion, as if it were his last living move. Then, with a fury, the whole mass uncoiled and exploded with such speed and force that the wire snapped like a rifle shot. Bulldog tried to hang on, but the rubber grip on the gaff pole parted, leaving Bulldog holding nothing but the rubber. Stunned, Bulldog and Bo watched yellow blood turn black as it curled and smoked around the now lifeless body. The big fish lay suspended, and then began to sink slowly. It was 15 feet under the surface and headed for where it had lived.

WHOOSH! SPLASH! Darcy made a perfect dive into the water. Bo and Bulldog watched, stunned and shocked even more. She let out a stream of bubbles as she swam deeper and deeper, chasing the fish. At 25 feet she caught up with the gaff rod and grabbed it. She struggled for the surface, her long legs biting into the water like a propeller. They watched in amazement as she actually made progress. It had been two whole forever minutes, and then her head finally broke the surface.

"Get him, Bo!" she screamed with the last of the breath in her. Bulldog grabbed the gaff rod from her and hurled the whole mess on the deck with a vengeance.

Bo reached down under Darcy's arms and hauled her as gently and quickly as he could into the cockpit.

"Are you all right, darlin'?"

She couldn't speak. All the air she could suck down was being used for more important things, like critical organ functions. He carried her into the salon and laid her carefully on the floor. Scared, he cradled her head in his arms. Her desperate breathing convulsions began to slow and become more normal. Bo just rocked her, thinking she was in as good a shape inside as she was outside.

Bulldog watched on.

"That was the damnedest thing I ever saw, Boss."

"I know, Bull. This one's as amazing as that creature laying out there on the deck."

"Awright, sonny boy, let's cut him." Darcy was out of his arms and headed for the cockpit. Before Bo could do or say anything, she had the knife in her hands and was down on her knees over the fish. She began furiously sawing and slicing under and between the gills. In a matter of seconds, she had the tough gizzard mass in her hands. The whole scene reminded Bo of an Aztec sacrifice when the chief cuts open the young virgin and holds the bloody heart up as an offering to the gods. Except he knew Darcy wasn't going to offer this to anybody. It was hers and she wanted it *real* bad.

She hacked open the tissue mass like she was hacking open a coconut. Digging in, she pulled the nugget treasure from the center. She clutched it with both hands and held it to her chest. Yellow blood ran down and pooled between her boobs. Bo and Bulldog watched speechless and frozen. She broke the ice.

"We're in the money now! Ten fucking roger, boys?"

"Ten roger," both said in unison.

"Hose this shit off me, Bulldog. Bo, get that faggot rum. It's *party* time."

They both blindly followed the orders. This gal could kick ass. Don't argue. Rum was poured. High fives went around. Rum was toasted. High fives again. Rum was drunk. *Full Bloom* was headed for the hill after another successful trip.

Bo turned to Darcy. "That was a hell of a thing you did back there. Weren't you scared?"

"I ain't scared of shit. Get past the fear of death and that's the death of fear."

Bo said nothing, but as he looked at her, he thought, I'll be a sonofabitch.

CHAPTER 19

Atom was walking slowly down the hospital corridor. He had just come from his daily visit with his niece, Julia. There was a lump in his throat. Her condition was worsening faster than anyone had predicted.

He didn't even remember driving through the Atlanta traffic back to his lab at Georgia Tech. Sitting numb at his desk, he found himself juggling the gold nugget from one hand to the other. He grabbed some metal snips from his drawer and tore a little chunk from the nugget and stuck it his pocket. He couldn't think, so he couldn't work, and decided to go home.

A mile from his house he pulled into Atlanta's biggest jewelry store. Digging through the six multi-colored pens in his plastic pocket protector, he pulled out the little chunk of gold.

"Could you make a starfish out of this?" Atom asked the jeweler. The jeweler whipped down his magnifying eyepiece and examined the chunk.

"Where did you get this?"

"Can you shape it into a starfish?"

"Why, yes, but I have manufactured gold starfish over there and it would be less expensive than making one with this."

"I want it made out of this gold," Atom said firmly. "How long?"

"Again, money sets the pace."

"Tomorrow, before noon."

"$500."

"Fine. Put it on a gold necklace like a charm, a good luck charm. See you tomorrow."

———————◆◆———————

Atom had the little box all wrapped up and behind his back when he walked into Julia's room. As he got close to the bed, he revealed the little present.

"Surprise!"

Julia took no time getting into it.

"A starfish! It's just like the ones Cap'n Bo and me always have races with."

"That's right, and this one is even *more* special. The gold came from Bo, so it's kind of his present to you, too."

Atom put it around her neck and clasped for her. They talked about the Bahamas, starfish, the pink sand, and the azure water. She made Atom promise to take her back down as soon as she felt better, and the promise broke Atom's heart because he knew it would never happen. After thirty minutes she was sleepy again and Atom left, with a kiss and a promise he could keep - to see her the next day.

A week passed, and every day Atom visited Julia. He had no children and Julia was his sister's only daughter. Atom had treated her as his own from the day she was born. It was the only child he had to love, and he did, very deeply. The nurse walked in.

"Hi, Atom. Hi, Julia. Here's lunch, sweetheart."

"Goodie. I'm hungry."

"You know, Atom, the last few days her appetite has soared."

"You're right and she has gotten more color lately."

"I'm glad. Got to run. There are more hungry ones down the hall."

Atom sat with her while she ate, kissed her, then left. He was still sad because he knew the inevitable, but at the same time he was happy she was feeling better. He suffered when she suffered.

Two weeks later the personal phone line on Atom's desk rang.

"Atom. Jane. How are you doing?" It was Dr. Jane Daniel, one of the country's leading pediatric leukemia physicians. "Atom, I just personally ran a second blood test on Julia because the first one the nurse ran was too unbelievable. My test came out just as unbelievable. Her hematocrit is up; the white blood count is up; the reds are much better shaped. All in all, I have never seen such a turnaround in my life. I don't want to give you false hopes, but something is going on that I just don't understand."

"Jane, by all accounts and all the specialists, she is, was, terminal. Are you saying now that may *not* be the case?"

"If the rapidity of this improvement maintains, there is hope, Atom. Look, when she was first diagnosed, you jumped into this and probably know more about the disease than most specialists. You're one of the country's most brilliant physicists. You help me figure it out."

"I will, Jane, and I've already got a lead. I'll see you this afternoon."

Atom flung open the desk drawer, got the snips out and carved two more little chunks of gold. He raced down the back stairs, leaping whole flights at a time. Fifteen minutes later he was standing in front of the jeweler.

"More starfish?"

"No. No time. Just anything to resemble a charm. I need them now. Hyper-speed. Got it?"

"I've got some stock dies back there. I'll just stamp something."

One hour later Atom was at the hospital. On Julia's hall there were several pediatric leukemia patients, and Atom asked Jane to put the necklaces on the two who were the most critically ill.

"What are these?" asked Jane.

"Gold fish parts," replied Atom with a wink.

From his car phone, he dialed his friend at the Department of

Energy, reserving the next available time slot on the National Accelerator, where he had privileges. Once that was nailed, he called his travel agent to book a flight. Two days later his plane touched down in Los Alamos.

Two assistants were assigned to Atom. He went over the game plan with them. They were going to plasmatize a known controlled gold sample and produce patterns as a result of collisions with ions. Naturally occurring gold is gold 197, meaning the atoms contain 119 neutrons and 78 protons. They were going to use the cyclotron to slam ions into the gold. The collision would take place at nearly the speed of light. Everything would act differently after the collision, depending on the atomic structure inherent in the sample. It's the manner and direction that the parts fly off that determines the material's innermost properties and secrets.

The first tests were on naturally occurring gold, and the resultant patterns were what Atom had expected. Bo's gold was next. After several hours of preparation, the test was ready to run.

"Son of an asteroid," Atom whispered to himself and the assistants.

"Observe how many additional neutrons this sample spun off. There have got to be at least five or six. Get the natural gold results and run them through the digital scanner. Let the computer tabulate the neutrons accurately. Then perform the same experiment with this material. I'll gander a wager of a new Teflon pocket protector on at least five more neutrons. Any takers?"

"No sir, professor. This shouldn't take long. By the way, where did you get this stuff?"

"Out of a fish."

"Yeah, right. A goldfish, doc?"

"You could say that."

Atom studied the patterns. Gold 202, *wow*! He twisted and turned the patterns, trying to force them to reveal more. When that didn't work, he twisted and turned his face instead. There was something else and he knew it. He wasn't quite ready to write with his indelible pen yet. He went over to the copier and made a clear copy of the Bo gold, and another clear copy of the standard gold sample. Overlaying the two, he placed them on the light table and began rotating them. He studied the combinations of patterns for an hour.

"Einstein utopia! Entropy! Elegant! An anti-anti-quark! Which is not two negatives creating a positive but it is a whole new sub-quark by itself. For the love of lasers!" Atom marveled to himself.

"Shut down and clean up for me, please, guys. I have to catch the next plane back to Atlanta, proton pronto fast. See you guys next time. Thanks." Atom was out the door with his cardigan sweater half on and his hushpuppies scurrying.

CHAPTER 20

Bo was standing in the telephone booth on the corner. It was a booth, but the phone was a regular old-fashioned, rotary desk phone propped up on a board that used to be one of Uncle Ulmer's signs. It only worked about every fourth day and this was it. A collect call to Atom was the business of the day.

"Bo, it's been four weeks since I've talked to you. What the Doppler is going on?"

"I'm sorry, Atom, but I've been real busy, and most of the time this phone doesn't work. Cora Lee's has been out, too. Plus, fish all night, sleep all day, you know."

"Well, how are things progressing?"

"We've been averaging ten fish a week, and that's a seven-day week, too. No matter what we do or try, we just can't seem to get any more. But I've measured 160 ounces."

"That's ... "

"Don't say it on this phone. I know prices and can multiply."

"Okay, I understand. Look, there is something very interesting going on. The sample has some unusual properties that may, and I repeat *may*, be helping Julia."

"Is she all right?"

"Yes, yes. That's what I'm saying. I fashioned a charm from a snippet of the first nugget, and Julia has been wearing it around her neck for weeks. Her blood work is showing a remarkable turnaround."

"I don't understand, but that's great."

"I am testing some additional charms on some other children, as we speak. Then I will be in a position to ascertain the results. Then, posthaste, I will be coming down. I cannot fish, however, because I will only be there a day."

"Good. We need to talk. I'll see you when you get here."

Bo headed back down the breezeway in a good mood. He had reason to be happy. Julia's getting better; the gold's coming, not great but steady; sex with Darcy was coming, great and steady; and it was a beautiful day in the Bahamas.

As he passed the bar and several people milling around, Darcy yelled, "Hey, Bo baby. Come have a smash."

"No, not now. I've got some stuff to do on the boat."

"All right, you little shit. I'm going to the beach after I drink this. See ya."

She kissed him on the cheek. He touched his cheek. She had never shown any affection in public. The day was even better.

"Have fun."

The big, sportfishing Post that Bo had admired weeks before was back across the dock. The crew pretty much kept to themselves and weren't very friendly. Bo had seen it before among a few of the crews in the sportfishing crowd. Big game fishing is so competitive, the new ones to the sport are intimidated by the veterans. Bo was more than a veteran; he was almost a legend.

Bo had a feeling about that crew and owner that he just couldn't nail, but it was there, and it wasn't a good feeling. They seemed to be up to something. Bo had never seen them fish, and maybe that was what was fishy.

"Buy you another drink?" the Post captain offered Darcy, sitting at the bar.

"Eat shit. I can buy my own friggin' drink."

"Girl's got an attitude," the mate said.

"Do you know what boat we are on?"

"It's plastered all over your fuckin' shirt. What does *Onrop* mean, any fuckin' way?"

"The owner likes it. I don't know. The owner is looking for one more crew. See, it's just Mike here and me, and he's looking for a woman to manage the inside."

"I used to be a professional server, ya know."

"I didn't know that, but it's good to know now. The owner can be an asshole sometimes, but he pays so well Mike and I put up with it."

"What does he pay that's so hot?"

"Well, last week we were back in Palm Beach. He bought me a brand new black Jaguar, just out of nowhere. I asked him why, and he just said he appreciated the way I managed the boat. Hell, he bought Mike here a new Harley."

"That's pretty cool. You mean a *brand* new Jag?"

"Yeah. He gives us stuff all the time. Shit, he pays Mike here three hundred."

"Three hundred a week is what I made slinging whiskey."

"Three hundred a day, sweetheart."

"Jeez. What will he pay to take care of the inside?"

"At least the three hundred. Hell, someone like you would get plenty of goodies like cars and jewelry and diamonds. Easy, girl."

"I'll think about it. Hey, this guy doesn't like peanut butter and jelly sandwiches, does he?

"No. Why?"

"Nothing. I got to go the beach and get some sun. Bye."

"We'll be around."

Darcy threw her beach bag over her shoulder and strolled off thinking, cars, jewelry, diamonds.

"Good job, Dave. She's hooked. She's also gorgeous. It's too bad we gotta just use her and dump her. Hey, maybe the boss will try her in a flick," Mike said.

"I doubt that girl would do a flick. With her bad ass attitude she'd be good in a war picture, though."

On the pink sand, Darcy had spread a big, white towel with dark blue *Full Bloom* embroidered on the bottom. Bo had told her not to take those towels to the beach; they were used only for decoration on special occasions. But she had worked hard and figured she deserved it.

Her ritual was precise and practiced. She took great care and effort to lay the towel just right, flat, fully spread, and facing the full angle of the sun. It was done with the same great care that Bo treated his baits. Darcy laid on the towel the same way the towel was put down, flat, fully spread, and facing full to the sun. The spreading part was to expose those parts that normally didn't get sun from just living, just walking around. She spread her fingers to let the sun do its job between them, even her toes, too. Bo couldn't figure how she had that much muscle control to spread her toes. He had tried, just as a joke, to demonstrate how silly it was. He couldn't do it. Darcy seriously told him it was years of patient practice born of necessity.

She was almost entering that other world of blissful peace when: drop, drop, drop; cool water dripped on her stomach.

"What the hell!" she screamed, bolting straight up to see a black Bahamian boy waddling off as fast as he could.

"Come here, you dumb little shit!" she commanded. He stopped, turned, and slowly waddled back. He was as fat as a blowfish and as black as diesel oil. At four feet high and four feet around, he was proportional to Bulldog. Dangling from each hand was some sort of fish with their tails dragging in the sand.

"What the hell did you do that for?" she demanded.

"Well ma'am, I ketch two, an I aimed to see if you wanted ones."

"That's the ugliest fish I ever saw. What the hell would I want it for?"

"Why, to eat, ma'am. Dis is da best eats in da ocean. It be a box fish."

He held one as high as he could, which only managed to clear the tail an inch off the ground, not that the fish was long; he was short. The box fish looked just like a box the size of a loaf of bread. Brown splotches covered a background color of mustard yellow. The snout slopped forward to a little parrot-like beak of a mouth. Tiny fins were attached to either side and the tail was not much bigger. It twitched a little just at the base like a cocker spaniel's snubbed tail wags. This fish was not a great hunter of the sea but a reef dweller, picking and pecking its way through life.

"Eat *that*?"

"Yes ma'am. We in dese waters name him 'chicken o da sea' sincin he tastes same as da chicken do."

"It *all* tastes like chicken, sonny."

"Well, is da best an ... I just taught, well ... " He was turning to leave.

"Wait. How old are you?"

"Twelve, ma'am," he said proudly.

"And you caught those all by yourself?"

"Yes ma'am!" even more proud.

"Where?"

"Why, ma'am, da reef be right dare." He pointed out to where turquoise water boiled into brown over the coral heads.

"How do you catch these rascals anyway?"

"Wit dis hook." He dug in his pocket and produced an old rusty hook tied to a balled up piece of line.

"Most peoples dey have a hard time, doe. I been watchin' deez fish all my life an dey be mighty picky to gets dem to bite an den if you don't snatch em just at da very second before dey bites dey can pick you clean. I knows. I been studyin' a long time. I knows." He was getting excited, sharing his secrets with someone.

"You're pretty smart."

"Nooo, ma'am. You even call me dumb. Dey all call me dumb. I tink causin I fat, dey tink I dumb."

"I didn't mean it that way. You don't act dumb."

"Yes, ma'am, I do. I do. I do dumb tings so dey will laugh, so dey will take me along. My momma say it become da habit."

"Well that's dumb to *act* dumb. Why do you care?"

"Don you care?"

"I don't give a shit. Sorry. No."

"Yes, you do."

"No, I don't!"

"Yes, you do! I seen you on dis beach all de time."

"So? What of it?"

"Why you here?"

"To get sun. Shit, I'm arguing with a twelve-year old."

"Why you get de sun?"

"To get a tan. This is going nowhere, sonny."

"You come to de beach to lays out in de sun, to gets a tan, cause you tink dat makes you look better, an you tells me you don care? You do cares what day tink. Just like me."

Darcy didn't say anything. She just looked out at the reef. The boy's eyes followed. He sat quietly, too. The box fish sat between them just as quiet. A cloud cast its shadow. Silence.

Five minutes later the cloud had passed, and Darcy said, "I've acted dumb, too."

"Why you? You so pretty. I act dumb cause I fat and ugly. You so pretty, you don have to."

"I'm not sure why. Isn't that something? I play dumb because I'm pretty and you play dumb cause you *think* you're ugly. Maybe because I am pretty that's all people expect from me. Look pretty, Darcy. Play the part they gave you, not your own. Shit! I believed them. You can't be anything else, so I'm not."

"Yeah. I fat so I can be no ting other either. Can't do ... so be dumb. I can't run to keep up with dem, so I swim in da ocean by myself. I can swim doe. In da water I float and can move like de porpoise. Dats where I gets to play my ownest part, by myself, in da ocean, dats my place."

"You're lucky. I don't have a place."

"Well, ma'am, I gots to get dese fish on da ice. I take you fish to my Momma. You knows Miss Sara?"

"Sure. You're Sara's boy? What's your name?"

"Archibald, Archie fa' short. You come roun bout six an Momma will show you da fixin of da box fish."

"I will, Archie. I sure will."

"An, ma'am?"

"Darcy."

"Miss Darcy, you *will* find de place, an it's not *under* dis sun. It's when you *shine* like da sun."

CHAPTER 21

A week later Atom climbed out of the water taxi and walked seriously down the dock, even though he was in another ridiculous outfit.

"Cool threads, Atom," Darcy greeted him from the cockpit.

"Hi, Darcy. You've become a real fisherman by now, right?"

"I'm with the best of 'em Atom, old boy, but I'm really a gold-digger."

"That stuff might be more than gold."

"Nothin's more than gold, you little psychic."

"Physics, Darcy, physics."

"Whatever. Go on in. Bo's inside fixin' the head again. I'm goin' to the beach."

Atom went in as Bo was coming out of the head, cussing.

"Hey, Atom," Bo said, scanning him. Where in the hell does he buy those clothes?

"Bo, how are you?" Atom said, shaking his hand.

"Wanna beer? You sound kinda serious."

"Yes, please, thanks. Bo, I've got some great news."

"I know. I've got a good maybe $70,000 in gold so far."

"Julia's getting better and better everyday."

"That's terrific, Atom. She's such a sweetheart."

"Bo, I haven't proven it yet, but you know when my gut tells me something about anything scientific, my head usually catches up, and it turns out to be true. I have never had a stronger premonition. The gold from those fish contains five extra neutrons, making it very radioactive. That's the part I know."

"That stuff going to make us glow like the lures?"

"No, the radioactivity has simply become a delivery mechanism. There is another phenomenon happening involving quarks. This particular brand of quarks, if you will, has an effect on the leukemia cells. It's literally transforming them into healthy, robust cells. I am not sure how, yet, but I know it's happening. That gold is saving Julia's life."

"Fantastic. This is some wild stuff. But what did you do?"

"As I told you, I fashioned a lucky charm out of the gold for Julia. I could have just bought her something in the store, but knowing how fond she is of you, I decided to use a snippet of your gold as something *extra* special. I put the charm on a necklace, and it rests right around the upper chamber of her heart. The body's entire blood volume is turned over right there every three minutes. Through radioactivity, the quark enters cells and then is deposited into the bone marrow. This stimulates healthy new cell growth. Again, I haven't proven anything yet, but I know in my gut it works. You know me, Bo. I'll find out why. I can't stand to *not* understand."

"How long will she have to wear it? I mean, does it cure her and then she can give it to another kid?"

"I do not know that, either. It's possible once she's healthy, she can. However, on the other hand, she may have to wear it all her life."

This conversation seemed too business-like. It wasn't like the good time talk when fishing. Something else was going on, and Bo sensed it and it made him uncomfortable.

"What are you going to do now?"

"Where is the gold?"

"Bulldog's been burying it like a dog in his backyard."

"I need it. All of it."

"What?"

"Bo, I *need* that gold. There are a lot of children with Julia's disease. We can save their lives."

"You're out of your friggin' mind, man! That gold is gonna get me out of debt, and then buy me a better boat, bigger bimbos, I mean bigger boat and better bimbos. Shit, damn, shit, what are you saying?"

"I'm saying I want to save children's lives, Bo. *That's* what I'm saying."

"No way, man. No friggin' way. I've worked too hard all my goddamned life for this and I ain't gonna give it up now. No friggin' way."

"I can't believe this. Bo, I thought I knew you, but I just don't believe this. You are so selfish you would allow children to die so you can have a bigger boat? Is it that girl? Has she got you so wrapped up you've become a gold-digger as well? Where is your conscience? Do you have a heart? Who are you, Bo?"

"Get the fuck out of here, asshole!" Bo shouted.

"I will. I better, because the current company I am in the presence of is likely to be struck by lightning any micro-second."

Atom didn't slam the door behind him; he didn't even close it. He just walked out and down the dock. Bo sat on the sofa holding his head in his hands. He sat there a long time.

"I gotta go talk to Uncle Ulmer," he said to himself. He was shocked, confused. Flip Flop.

CHAPTER 22

Uncle Ulmer was lying in his hammock, buried in the bushes of his corner, occasionally sipping from a Styrofoam cup. The stuff in the cup was industrial strength and was weeping through the cup, leaving little sweat beads of brown liquid on the outside.

"Ulmer! You in there?" Bo yelled, his eyes piercing into the brush.

"Bo. Cap'n Bo. My main mon! Come on in here. Lovely day to flat out, eh?"

"Ulmer, I've got a problem, and I need to know what you think."

"Bo, you know what I tink. You just need to hear me say it."

"Ulmer, I've got some stuff that could make me a lot of money."

"You back off 'en any ting to do wit dope now."

"No, it's not dope. It's legal. The problem is the stuff can help sick children, too. You know Atom?"

"Yeah. Hows be da lil' egghead?"

"Fine. Fine, but Atom's got a niece that's sick. Actually, she has leukemia."

"Dat's a large shame."

"Yeah it is, but this stuff I've got seems to cure her."

"Dats marvyloss! How much of de stuff you got?"

"Pretty good bit. I feel I should ... I don't know. The fact is, shit. The truth is ... damn!"

"I knows de problem now, Bo. If you tink moneys byside de lil uns you know what I tink. You know luki kema be da problem with da middle side of de bones. Do ya?"

"How in the hell do you know that?"

"Voodoo, mon. We in voodoo do da bone work all de time. Dats da main line. De bones, Bo, de bones, dey know. Why you tink we rattle dem chickens bones? Why you tink we hang dem chicken feet? Cause dey de bones, Bo. De bones is what dey dig up. De bones is dat ting that lasts."

Bo knew he was being lectured to, but he knew that's why he came.

"You can up them feelins all you can care to, Bo; you can tink all you can tink, but in those bones is where de real truth can be found. All the feelins in de world, dey be one ting, an all the mind games in de world, dey can be de other. But the real story be told in de bones, mon. De truth will set you free dey say. De truth be onliest in you head. Feelins ain't factses, Bo."

"De truth show hisself like a mornin' mist. You cain't see, so de bones rattle so you can follow. De real truth be not what you tink but what you does. But beyond dat, Bo, not what you does, but what da other peoples does cause what you does *first*. Voodoo, it starts in de heart and goes ups to de mind, but lives down in de bones. De bones put all in 'spective. What your bones tell you now, Bo?"

"Not much, but my mind tells me to ... "

"Then you ain't there yet, Bo."

"But!"

You gonna know when it happen. De bad ting; you cain't make it come. But Bo, de good ting - an dis is da good ting - when it comes you cain't make it go away neither. Do da right ting, Bo, an you bones will hold you up skraight an' proud. Do da wrong ting an your bones will turn to dust. Wanna beer?"

CHAPTER 23

Bo was sitting in the captain's chair with his feet propped up and not even drinking. He was thinking; thinking about Julia, about what Atom had said and about what Ulmer had just professed. Damn, he thought. Why does it always have to be so complicated? Why can't it just be simple? Let me catch fish, get the gold, sell the gold, buy a bigger boat, and play with the bimbos. Now all this moral shit rears its stupid head. I know what I ought to do, but I need the money, bad, real bad. I'm glad Julia's better. There are more Julias. Darcy won't like it, that I know

"Bo baby!" Darcy hollered as she jumped into the boat and started to climb the ladder. Thud.

"What's up? Where's Atom? Why do you look so fuckin' down?"

Bo said nothing.

"Earth to asshole. Earth to asshole."

"I'm thinking about giving the gold away!" Bo just blurted it out. He didn't mean to do it that way. It just came out.

"WHAT!?"

"I'm thinking of giving the gold away." This time he said it very quietly.

"What are you talking about?"

"Atom said the gold is different. Atom said the gold cures children's leukemia. Atom said it could cure more children. Uncle Ulmer said I ought to do it. I said I ought to, too."

"You're a lying sonofabitch!"

"Lying, about what?"

"You want that gold all to your asshole self. You think if you and Atom can come up with this shit story, I'll believe it, and everything will be just peachy keen. I'm not as fucking dumb as you think. Well, you and that psycho ain't cheatin' me out of diddly."

"Darcy, nobody's tryin' to cheat you. It's for a cause. Jeez, I hate that 'for a cause.' No, it's really to help some children. Atom's not sure. Atom is sure. He just can't prove it yet, but he will. Atom always does."

"I don't believe any of this crap. You used me. You don't want to share any fuckin' thing. You just want it all to yourself. You don't plan to give anything away, except me. You really think I'm that stupid, don't you, butthead?"

"No, it's true. It can help children. Besides, I haven't decided what to do. I said I was only *thinking* about it."

Pissed, she jumped from the bridge to the cockpit in one leap.

"You could've just said 'fuck you dumbass' instead of that 'helping the children.' I can understand dumbass, I've heard it *many* times before!"

Dave and Mike were in the cockpit of *Onrop* listening to all of the explosions drifting over from *Full Bloom*.

"Let's move, Mike. Here's our chance."

"Hey, Darcy. Come on over. The boss would like to meet you."

"That job still open? I need some money. This lying SOB screwed me out of my gold," she screamed. "Bo butt, these guys *pay*; you don't."

Darcy jumped on their boat, and the hairy frog owner came out of the salon, out from under a *willy* pad, tongue like a snake.

"Hey, darling." He came up to her and removed five gold chains from his thick, frog neck and put them around Darcy's neck.

"See!" she yelled across the dock. "I can get all the gold I want, Butthole! Screw your children's gold, you ... you lying son-ofabitch!"

John Bloomfield

Bo could only watch. He hadn't figured on any of this. He was confused. All this had happened too fast. It was out of control.

"Darcy. I only said I was *thinking*, not doing."

"Dave, crank her up and let's get out of here fast, before these two lovebirds change their minds."

"Aye, aye, to that!"

The big diesels roared to life. Mike was fast with the lines, so fast it looked as if he could untie and go away a hell of a lot faster than they could come in and tie up. Escape artist, practice makes perfect. As they pulled away from the dock, Bo could only watch, speechless.

"Bye, Bo! You asshole! One more thing! I'll be back one day and I'm gonna screw you to the goddamned wall just like you done me, and that's one promise I'll die tryin' to keep," she screamed over the engines.

Bo had said good-bye before, but he had never had good-bye said to him. The *staying* side of good-bye was new to him and he didn't like it. It hurt.

Once out of the harbour, the big sportfisherman steamed south. Comfortable in the huge salon sat Darcy, the frog owner, and some hunk guy named Peter. Sitting on soft leather with a Bloody Mary in hand and gold around her neck, Darcy was feeling pretty good, although she was still pissed.

"So, darling, how long have you been on the island?"

"About two months."

"And that Cap'n Bo, I hear he's a pretty good fisherman."

"He's the best, that lying asshole."

"What did he lie to you about, Darling?"

"About giving the go ... ," she caught herself in time.

"Giving what?"

"Nothing."

"You guys go out at night to fish, don't you?"

"Sometimes. What the fuck is this, some sort of interview?"

"No, darling, no. I'm just interested, just talking. What do you catch with those mega electric reels anyway?"

"Get me another drink." Darcy wanted to change the subject. The hunk, Peter, took her glass and proceeded to oblige her.

"What do you want out of life?" The frog owner had asked this stock question often. It usually worked because once these girls' material dreams were known, he would then promise to make their dreams come true. He was the one who could deliver. They always told him, and they were always material, and he always promised.

"I want a bright red BMW convertible with red nails to match and a penthouse in Palm Beach." The frog almost croaked, he had heard that one a hundred times before. Why couldn't they come up with something different once in a while?

"Work for me and all that can be yours."

"Well, I am a professional server, you know. I can take real good care of you guys around here."

"That's great, darling."

"By the way what the hell does this boat name *Onrop* mean?"

"It's Porno spelled backwards."

Darcy was looking at her flip-flops, working the letters in her mind. Then she caught on to what was going on. She had it figured out, Peter and all.

"Mister, if you think I'm gonna do any of that shit, you might as well take this boat and stuff it up your ugly ass. And for you, Mr. Peter, you keep your peter in your pants cause if I see it, I'll rip it off and cram it down your pretty throat. Ten Fucking Roger?"

She bolted for the door and scampered to the foredeck. As soon as this boat hits a dock I'm off, she vowed to herself. Hell, I'm getting *real* good at jumping ship.

"Boss, you want me to go get her?" Peter said.

"No, we've done mock rape pornos before and they didn't sell worth a shit. No sense in trying a real one. Anyway, what I really want from her is to find out what the hell they're up to out there. I got a feeling there's bucks in the deal."

———•———

Night came and they were still steaming south. Darcy was still alone on the foredeck. The frog came around the corner.

"Hi, darling. Don't be afraid."

"I'm not afraid of your ugly ass."

"Well, I'm not going to ask you to do anything. I just thought you might be thirsty. Here." He handed her a can of Coke, already open with a straw in it.

"I'll leave now. Be careful out here."

Darcy was thirsty. She threw the sissy stick away and turned the can up, taking big gulps. It didn't take five minutes before her legs crumbled beneath her. They were waiting to drag her back into the salon. She could see and she was awake, but she had no control; she actually felt peaceful. The figures in her vision were blurred and moved in slow motion, ghost like.

"Prop her up on the sofa, guys. All right. Darcy, you go fishing at night with Cap'n Bo, don't you?

"Yes."

"What do you catch when you go fishing?"

"Fish."

"Oh, man," Dave said.

"What kind of fish, Darcy?"

"Gold fish."

"There are no goldfish out there. Why do you call them goldfish?"

"Because there's gold in them, you dumb shit."

"She just doesn't quit, does she, Boss?"

"Let me get this straight. You catch fish with gold in them?"

"Yes." She passed out.

"Shit. She drank that stuff too fast."

"There's no fish with gold in it, but I think the little whore is right about the gold part. Back in the 1850s a huge schooner was coming from San Francisco loaded with gold bullion for the Confederate side. In a hurricane it sank somewhere off Eleuthera. That much I'm sure of.

"Mel Fisher, the guy who found the *Attocia* and raked in a billion dollars worth of gold, looked for it for years and never did find it. I'll bet you that guy's found it. At any rate, we're going to find out, too. Dave, call the pilots on the secure satellite phone. Tell them to get Guido and a couple of goons over to - where we going?"

"San Salvador."

"San Salvador. Tell them to get here tomorrow. Is our rubber tender up and going?"

"Yes, sir."

"When they get here, plan to head back to Harbour Island. Tomorrow night Guido's going to pay the *Full Bloom* a little visit."

"Yes, sir!"

CHAPTER 24

Darcy woke to darkness. The glow from the hidden valance lights provided just enough light to see. She didn't move; she moved her eyes. I've got to get off this boat, she said to herself. She quietly stood and tested her legs. They were wobbly, but okay. She could tell the boat was tied up. She moved to the door and on the count of three, flung it open. It only took her two strides to cross the cockpit and one jump off the covering boards to clear the ten feet to the dock. She was off to the races now.

"Hey!" someone yelled from the boat. Flip-flops flip-flopped in record cadence. After a mile or so, she saw a sign for Riding Rock Inn. Beside the little office was a banyan tree with its branches hanging low. It was the safety umbrella she needed. Underneath, Darcy hid and sat with her legs tucked to her chest, waiting out the rest of the night.

It was later than she thought, because dawn came quickly. But what to do now? She heard the puttering of a moped coming down the road. A little old Bahamian man pulled up wearing a plastic hard hat with BaTelCo, Bahamian Telephone Company, emblazoned across the front. Darcy thought, well at least there is *one* phone here, probably broken. She got up and approached him.

"Excuse me, sir. Is there an airport on this island?"

"Why yes, chil'. Dares one."

"Where is it?"

"Down' de road a piece."

"Will that thing hold both of us, so you can take me there?"

"Yes, chil', it will carry two. I can'ts doe. Dis scoot be BaTelCo property an is again da rule."

Darcy yanked one of the gold necklaces off and offered it.

"Here. This will break the rule."

"Get on, chil'."

They puttered off, almost squashing the moped. The sight was curious, a gorgeous girl with blond hair streaming in the breeze, hanging onto an old, little, black Bahamian man with a grizzled gray beard, dodging potholes on this sputtering, under-powered bike. Darcy thought, if Mom could see me now! She was going home.

The airport was a red-painted, open shed, no more than 15 by 15 feet. There were no chairs, only benches nailed to the walls. No counter or check-in existed. One lonely Cessna 410 sat on the pitted ramp, with two pilots performing a pre-flight. The plane was pretty beat up and was used to haul island freight. Darcy walked up with her best walk, all things considered.

"Hi, guys."

"Hi to you, beautiful."

She smiled.

"What on the earth is a girl like you doing on a desolate rock like this?"

"Actually, I don't know. I'm trying to get off. Where you headed?"

"Back to Lauderdale."

"I need a ride."

"I guess we can. Go get your stuff."

"I don't have any stuff. This is it."

"Passport, money, nothing? Are you a U.S. citizen?"

"Yeah, born and raised in Lauderdale."

"How do you expect to prove that to Immigration when we get there?" She just shrugged. He turned to his co-pilot.

"We can't do this. I really am not into smuggling aliens."

Darcy ripped off her four remaining gold chains.

"Here."

"Damn, she's desperate. If we go into Executive Airport instead of International, we could pull it off."

"All right. Look, when we get there, you go straight to the ladies room. We'll cause some confusion with the plane. You jump out the window and you're on your own then. Okay?"

"Ten roger."

The plane bounced and skipped over the World War II pavement. Then it escaped. Darcy sat on a mailbag, looking out the window. She had no gold left, but at least she was headed home.

CHAPTER 25

Silently, the three goons paddled the rubber tender. Dressed in black with survival knives strapped to their calves, each carried a 9 mm Glock pistol stuck in shoulder harnesses. They moved with a sense of purpose. They had a mission. There was no moon and the night was black, black except for the pool of green glow that suspended *Full Bloom.*

Bo and Bulldog were in the cockpit, waiting and ready for the first strike of the night. Jimmy Buffett provided the background. He was singing about a cheeseburger in paradise, while Bulldog ate one and in the same place, too. Bo was reading Hemingway's *Islands in the Stream* for the hundredth time. *Full Bloom* approached at a lazy one knot, as they maneuvered the rubber tender to intercept.

The rubber boat brushed gently against the hull, making no noise. They tied the tender to the anchor hanging under the bow pulpit and hoisted themselves one by one onto the bow of boat. With hand signals they double-checked the plan. Quietly edging down the sides of the cabin, two took to the starboard side, single file, and one took the port. When they got close to the cockpit they crouched. A second before the surprise attack *Full Bloom* lurched on a beam wave, and the guy on the port side had to grab the aluminum upright of the tower.

Bulldog saw the hand. Instinctively, and in fishing reaction mode, Bulldog clamped down on the wrist and flung with all his might. All Bo saw was a sprawled body, cartwheeling through the air over the cockpit and landing 15 feet behind the boat in the wake. Bo dove for the salon door and the rifle. As he did, the first guy on the starboard side came around and fired. *Islands in the Stream* exploded from Bo's hand. The guy was on top of him, and Bo could feel the cold steel of the pistol on his temple. He closed his eyes tight, waiting. Milliseconds were eternity. He heard nothing. Felt nothing. But he was sure it had happened, because all of a sudden the guy's 200-pound weight was off of him and he felt like he was floating.

He opened his eyes and looked up to see a body stuck clean through the chest with a flying gaff. Suspended six feet above him and dangling from Bulldog's arm, the man was wiggling and twitching like a frog freshly gigged on the end of a gig pole. Intestines were starting to pour out of him where his wiggling had caused the razor gaff to open him up. With one sweep Bulldog flung him, his guts, the flying gaff and the whole mess overboard.

POW! POW! POW! POW! POW! Five shots rang out as fast as a finger could pull a trigger. Bulldog staggered, then fell, smashing the teak back of the chair. He tumbled to the cockpit deck, pinning Bo with the weight of his legs alone. Bo could see the bright red circles forming on Bulldog's chest. The third goon stood over them, with his pistol pointed steady at Bo.

"What the fuck is going down here?" he asked with authority. Bo said nothing.

POW! The tackle drawer exploded behind Bo's head.

"Who the hell are you?"

POW! Another drawer exploded. Hooks rained down on them, tinkling like silverware falling from the sky.

"Kill me, asshole!" Bo shouted. "I don't give a shit. 'Cause if you don't, it's gonna be damn fun killing you.

"I'm paid to kill. That's what I do, little fella. I'll ask you one more time. What game are you pricks playing out here?"

"Fuck you."

"Well, well, tough guy. Maybe your fat, lard ass buddy ain't quite bought it yet. You know, maybe he's not so dead. You two a couple of faggots, huh? I bet you have a hard time finding his dick in all that fat, huh? Mutt and Jeff, just a regular ol' Mutt and Jeff scene. I'm going to make damn sure that fat faggot is dead dead."

He leveled the pistol at Bulldog's head.

"Wait! What do you want?"

"I want to know all about your little game out here."

Bo noticed the goon held himself steady against the rocking boat by holding on to the arm of the fighting chair. He also noticed Bulldog had left a secondary set of backup rigs in the chair. The wire that ran to the backup rod was brushing against the man's forearm.

"All right, asshole, I'll tell you," Bo said. "But let me get up from under his legs so I can breath." Bo started to work his way out from under Bulldog.

"That's more like it. Easy, real easy," the man said, as he grinned.

Bo put one hand on the steps and the other on the electric reel to pull himself up. His right thumb could feel the rubber booted toggle switch on the reel. One, two, three, FLIP. The reel took off in fast retrieve. The spare coil came off the chair, and the 6-inch barbed hook bit and dug deep into the goon's forearm.

As the first hook tore deeper and ripped up his arm, a second hook went right through his hand. He dropped the gun and grabbed at his arm, not knowing what the hell was happening. The big reel tore the eyes off the rod as it munched snaps and rigging. The goon had no choice but to follow his arm or have it ripped out like the snaps.

Bo scrambled to his feet fast. He lunged at him and knocked him overboard. With less than a foot of wire left, Bo killed the switch. Hung by the wire and his arm, the goon thrashed in the water like a wired sailfish. Bo turned animal, mad animal, rabid animal. He picked up the fish bat and thwacked him on the side of the head.

"Hush now, little fishy," Bo coaxed sadistically. The whack had stunned the attacker. Bo whipped his knife from his belt sheath and cut him in long deliberate strokes, just skin deep. The blood poured and swirled and turned black in the water. He snatched two ten-pound weights from the deck and calmly wired them to the hook stuck through the guy's hand. The crazed man came to and began thrashing again.

"It's tough stayin' on top of the food chain, pal. You're in my world out here with Mother Ocean. My world," Bo taunted him.

As he did, he loosened the drag on the reel and wire peeled off. Bo stopped it when his head was just above the water line. Terror was in his eyes. In only seconds the first shark nosed him, rolled sideways, membraned his eyes, peeled back lips, and tore at his dinner's leg. The screams jolted Bo out of his trance.

"Bull!" Bo turned and hit the deck on his knees next to Bulldog. He felt him all over like a police frisk, not knowing what else to do. He listened to his chest and heard nothing. He pried Bulldog's eyes open and saw white. Sea water splashed from thrashing sharks and screams filled the cockpit, but Bo was oblivious to it all. He flung the door off the locker and grabbed several lifejackets. He wedged the jackets around Bulldog's head and sides to keep him from rolling in an attempt to stabilize him.

"I've got to get him to Nassau. Please, God, please."

He scrambled to the bow and cut the line to the tender. Just as fast, he scrambled back to cut the wire from the rigs in the water. He had forgotten about the goon, until he looked over the side. Sharks were in a feeding frenzy over legs and arms and other body parts. Half the torso was gone, but the face was still there looking at him, staring with a last look of horrified surprise. First a wave of fear hit Bo; then the self preservation circuit of "take to the offense" clicked in, and, as he cut the wire, he said, "Bon apetit, Shark Mutt, Shark Jeff."

CHAPTER 26

Bo leapt up the ladder to the bridge. He white-knuckled the throttles and slammed them to the wall. *Full Bloom* roared and began to lurch from wave to wave as she picked up speed. Bo flicked the autopilot on and set it for 15 degrees to get around the bank and the islands of North Eleuthera. He was headed for Nassau.

"Dear God, don't let him be dead. Please, God. Let him be alive. Let him live. Please God." Bo had never prayed in his life, but he *knew* he was praying now. His words came up through him so deep he didn't even know where they came from.

"The best, kindest giant of a man to ever grace this hemisphere is in your hands, God. Why not *me*? All the shit I've done. All the people I've hurt. Why him? Why not me?" He went below and knelt next to Bulldog, just holding his head in his hands and snugging the lifejackets. That was all he could do. He felt so helpless.

"All this crap about gold and bigger boats and better bimbos. That's all I wanted," he said out loud. "What did you want? All you wanted was to buy Christmas for every kid on the island. And if you could get enough, you'd make it Christmas everyday. *Damn* my ass and *bless* your soul, buddy. In my greed, look what I've done. I'm sorry. I'm so sorry. Well, that's over now, buddy. Everything we got, and everything we will ever catch, will go all over the world for the children. Live, Bull. I need you. The kids need you. It's me and you, buddy. We got work to do. Ulmer was right; you can't make it come, but when it comes, you can't make it go away either. And that is the good thing. Please God!" Flip Flop.

Bo felt the beginnings of the sea coming around from the lee of the islands; he could turn the corner now. He went up top and course corrected to 220 degrees, dead bull's eye for Nassau.

"Come on, boat! Come on!" he yelled as pushed on throttles that could go no further. He looked at the speed log, and it read 35 knots. Thing's broken again, he thought. The Loran read the speed over ground as 34 knots. Bo looked down at the water. The ocean was rushing by him faster than he had ever seen *Full Bloom* go through it. The boat's 100 percent "theoretical" speed was 28 knots. What was happening?

"This is impossible," he muttered.

The revelation hit him. "Yes, God!" he yelled. He knew then that Bulldog was alive. *Full Bloom* could never go that fast. She was getting help, big time help. Bo knew in his heart that the hand that pushed the boat was the same hand that held Bulldog's life

"Nassau Harbour Club, this is the *Full Bloom*. Come back!" he yelled into the mike.

"Hell, who am I calling? It's two in the morning!"

"Nassau Marine Radio ... *Full Bloom*, come back"

"This is Nassau Radio, switch two-four, two-four"

Bo switched.

"Nassau Radio?"

"Go ahead."

"Listen very carefully. I have a seriously injured man on board. I'm at twenty-five ten latitude, and seventy-seven zero five longitude. I am thirty minutes from the dock at the Nassau Harbour Club. I need the best paramedic team on the island there now. I need the best surgical team on the island, scrubbed and waiting at the hospital. The nature of the injuries is gunshot. Cost is no object, understand? The injured party is the United States Ambassador to England. England! Got it? Any questions?"

"No, sir! Harbour Club face dock, now. Gunshot. Ambassador."

"You're good, whoever you are, and the Ambassador will personally thank you when he is well. Standing by sixteen, twenty-four."

Bo turned off the autopilot and gripped the wheel. When he rounded the corner and turned up the Nassau Harbour channel, he could see in the distance hundreds of red flashing lights. The word was out. Every red light that could rotate, swivel, blink, flash or plain turn on was there. He held the 35 knots until he was just a hundred yards from the dock. When he pulled back, the boat lurched forward on its own wake, then settled. Bo spun hard around, gunning reverse so hard the transmissions could be thrown slap out of the boat. Nobody ever docked a boat faster.

Bo killed the engines and kissed the wheel of the *Full Bloom*. Hands were there to help tie the boat up, and paramedics were already on board by the time Bo came off the bridge. Confusion broke out about how to carry a man so big, but Bo had already anticipated that. With line in hand, he lashed two gurneys together. It took eight men to carry the load. Bo climbed in the back of the ambulance and watched as the paramedics swiftly started IVs.

The hospital was only five minutes away and the team Bo had requested was ready. An army of orderlies muscled Bulldog into the operating room. Bo paced for a couple of minutes and then collapsed. Emotional overload had taken its toll. He had come close to dying, had killed a man, killed him viciously, even sadistically, while believing his best friend was dead. He had run a boat as he had never done before, all in a matter of a couple of hours. Two orderlies carried him to a room and laid him on a bed.

The sun had just moved; it streamed unencumbered through the slightly parted drapes. The spotlight woke Bo. He looked at his watch.

"Shit, it's 8 o'clock. Where am I?" He collected his wits, and out the door he flew. Halfway down the hall, he began yelling to the nurses' station, "How is he? How is he?"

A very distinguished-looking black doctor walked briskly to

meet him.

"Please sit down, sir," Dr. Hamilton, Chief of Surgery said to him, in perfect Queen's English.

"I can't sit! How is he?" Bo yelled.

Dr. Hamilton grabbed Bo by the shoulders, and firmly stated, "He's going to be fine, sir!"

The biggest grin came over Bo. He never knew he could grin like that, and almost felt self-conscious doing it.

"Now sit," Dr. Hamilton said.

"Your friend is fortunate he is so, shall we say, obese."

"He's a fat fucker, ain't he?" Bo gushed.

"So he is, sir. The multiple layers of tissue, fat, if you will, absorbed four of the rounds very handily."

"Better than a flak jacket, huh, Doc?"

"Yes, one might say that. However, one round pierced the apex of his heart. We had to excise, cut, considerable heart muscle to remove the round. In my opinion, he'll recover, but it will take some time."

"Can I see him now?"

"No. He will be sedated all day, but perhaps this evening. I do not intend to be rude, Captain, ah ... ."

"Bo."

"Captain Bo, but I must bid you a farewell for home. It's been a long night and I am very tired."

"You did a great job, Doctor, and I thank you. I owe you as many fishing trips as you want."

"Thank you, sir. By the way, I practiced medicine in England for fifteen years and that fellow is *not* the ambassador of anywhere."

"Is that what I said? What I meant was, he's Santa Claus," said Bo with a grin.

"And, oh, by the way, Captain Bo, he's got the biggest heart I've ever seen."

"I know, Doctor, I know." Bo said. "Thank you. Tight lines to ya."

They turned and walked in opposite directions down the hall.

Bo walked down Bay Street in his own world. He didn't notice the tourists, the street vendors, the straw merchants or the stores. He was on his way back to the boat to do Bulldog's chores because he wanted to, and he needed to. Bulldog's chores; clean the boat, the boat that saved his life, *Full Bloom*.

CHAPTER 27

The whole island was abuzz about the shooting. North Eleuthera police had convinced Nassau they could handle the investigation locally. Bo had his story and he was going to stick to it. The head honcho had called a meeting in the offices at the airport. Bo strolled past the doors of the yellow building and entered the white one that said Do Not Open. Inside were six officials. Bo knew all but two of them. The Customs guy was there, as well as the Immigration fellow. All of them were decked out in their best uniforms, their white shirts were even whiter against their black skin. The collars were stiffly starched, a formal hangover from the proper days of the English, but making absolutely no sense in 95 degree heat and 100 percent humidity. Black pants, blacker then their skin, were creased sharply and decorated with a two-inch wide red stripe all the way down the sides. Topping off the ensembles were shiny brass buttons everywhere.

This was a big deal for these parts, and he figured they all wanted a piece of the excitement. Bo wasn't going to disappoint them. They had borrowed a set of the different colored chairs from the airport waiting room for the occasion. Two reds, a blue, a green, and two yellows were lined up behind a folding table that required a crushed Coke can under one leg to maintain stability. A roach was fingering the opening with his antennae, but a steady line of obediently marching ants was in his way. He was probably pretty pissed off, Bo figured.

"Cap'n Bo. How are you? Please enjoy da seat." Mr. Cooper

gestured toward the solitary red chair facing the table, as they shuf-fled about to find their own places. Bo figured his red seat was the hot seat.

"How is Mate Bulldog dis day?"

"He is doing very well, thank you." Bo was touched that they led off with a concern for Bulldog, but then, everybody loved him.

"I guess you gentlemen have heard that over 300 children from Spanish Wells to Governors Harbour have signed a giant 'Get Well' card in the shape of a heart for him."

"Yes Cap'n, dat we did."

"Dat boy earnin' of it, too."

"Cap'n, do you know why we gather here dis day?"

"To pray for Bulldog's speedy recovery?"

"Dat true, but we on dis panel have a curiosity."

"What might that be, sir?"

"How dat boy got shot!"

"It is not a very long story, but it is long on weird."

"Well, let us begin."

One of the officers Bo did not know pulled out a tape recorder and placed it in the middle of the table. When he attempted to turn it on, it only screeched. Subsequent bangings of it on the table resulted in plastic components flying off and onto the floor. What was left, the man quietly put back in his pocket.

"You gentlemen are aware we are in the heart of the Bermuda Triangle?" Bo began.

"Dat we know."

"Over the years a lot of strange and weird things have happened around these islands, and I guess it was only a matter of time before something would happen to me. Bulldog and I were on the *Full Bloom*, six miles off the Glass Window, at about 11 o'clock at night."

"Please slow down, Cap'n." The man who had the tape recorder was now taking notes. Bo rocked back on his chair.

"We were tracking south, and from the north we saw a faint green, glowing light in the sky. Bulldog remarked he had never seen a green star. To tell you the truth, I never had either. Well, this green glow was getting bigger and bigger, like it was coming toward us. We were fishing, but we sure kept an eye on it. It took over a half an hour to get to us. About a mile away, we knew it was big. It just kind of hovered, about a hundred yards over the water."

Bo had them all leaning forward, their eyes getting bigger and bigger, commensurate with the story and the growing green glow. The note taker had quit his scribbling.

"At fifty yards behind the boat, it just stopped and hung there. Bulldog was waving a friendly hello, but I went for the Ruger. I threw in a thirty-round banana clip, chambered the first round, and commenced to firing, squeezing them off faster than auto. It was kind of a shoot-now, ask-questions-later thing. I had run off fifteen or twenty rounds when Bulldog grabbed the rifle from me. He said I shouldn't be shooting at folks I didn't know. I guess my shooting at them pissed them off, so they returned fire. Problem was, now Bulldog had the gun. They shot at him, not me, and as you know, hit him five times. Then 'Big Bad John' came blaring on the stereo and they sped off. I figure they either didn't like country music or they thought 'Big Bad John' was going to be too much to handle. I'd like your thoughts on that."

"Ah, I doesn't care for dat country music mysef."

"Me as well. Reggae dots tunes, you know."

"I 'greed."

"Gentlemens, dats not da point here. Dis is extremely hard to fathom."

"We were in two hundred fathoms, sir."

"Dat so?"

"Yes, sir. I know this is difficult, but this *is* the Bermuda Triangle. I have proof. When this thing was at five hundred yards, I shot this picture." Bo reached in his pocket and floated the picture on the table for all to see. Bo had taken a picture of the lure - out of focus, all fuzzy, green, torpedo-shaped, and glowing.

"Now dis is da proof gentlemens," the lead officer said, as the others rose out of their seats to get a closer look. Bo gave them time to marvel and mutter.

"Gentlemen, I have a deal for you," Bo announced and they all looked up.

"That picture is very valuable to papers like *The Enquirer, The Star, The Globe,* and stuff. If you guys just drop this whole thing, you can have the picture and sell it *and* the story to them."

"Just one moment please, Cap'n." They huddled in the corner like used car salesmen, considering. Bo gave them time again.

"Cap'n, you have a deal."

"Thank you."

They re-huddled and Bo could hear the pie being split. Bo split too. So had the cockroach.

CHAPTER 28

Bo went straight from the inquest to the dock at Valentine's. The news had beat him across the bay. He was covered up with people wanting to know the details, so he retreated to the boat for other cover. All he said was "no comment," which only succeeded in pouring more fuel on the fire. It sounded so official and added to the intrigue. Even *The Star* was going to have a hard time with this story after the Bahamians got through with it.

Looking out the window, he saw Benjamin Rutherford coming down the dock in a determined fashion. Bo knew he was coming to see him. The Rutherford family was one of the wealthiest families in the country. Ben's great-great-great grandfather owned all the railroads in the United States in the late 1800s. They were right in there with the likes of the Carnegies and the Rockefellers. He had started the Billfish Foundation, which promotes the release of billfish. Bo was an early member and supporter. At first he joined selfishly, figuring more fish, more charters, more money, but now he agreed with the principle. Ben and Bo had known and liked each other for years. When he got to the boat, Bo opened the door.

"Hey, Ben, get in here."

"What the hell is going on? How is Bulldog?" Ben started in on him before he was even in the cockpit.

"Want a beer?"

"Yeah."

"Come in and sit down. You won't believe what has happened in the last three months."

It took two hours and 12 beers to get it all out. Bo told him about the lure, even showed him one. He told him about the fish and the gold and even showed him one of the nuggets. The story went to Julia in Atlanta and the leukemia and the cure. Bo didn't know who the goons were but wasn't worried about them anymore. Bulldog was fine and recovering quickly.

In the end, Bo said, "I have made up my mind, Ben. I was close before Bull got shot, but thinking he was dead cinched it for me. I promised myself, and more so Bull, that the gold *will* go to the children."

"So forget the money?"

"Yeah, there really are more important things. Bet you thought you would never hear my ass say that."

"I wonder if there is more stuff out there that we don't know about that can be of medicinal help. Shit, there's got to be. You know, we call the Mother Ocean the last frontier. I am sure there is, aren't you?"

"I am sure, too, but it's going to take time to find, and time is money."

"I've got an idea, Bo, an interesting idea. I'm going to New York tomorrow for the Rutherford Foundation meeting and review. What if the Rutherford Foundation sets up an organization to fund more discoveries? It'll be for the benefit of humanity and that's what they're into. We could set it up right here on Briland." Ben was getting excited.

"You could continue to fish for the gold, but expand the operation."

"Yeah, Ben, but I've got to live on something."

"Damn, Bo, you don't get it. I'm sorry, I just don't think about money."

"I know. You were born with a silver spoon up your ass. I wish it had a hook in it, so I could yank the leader every once in a while and bring you down to the rest of us peons."

"What I mean is the foundation would pay you and Bulldog and expenses and everything. In fact, we've got to have a boat, so the new organization will buy *Full Bloom* for a fair price. Hell with fair price. *Double* what it's worth, so you can pay it off and put some dough in the bank. On top of that, we could give you and Bulldog a signing bonus, and insurance and pension plans and everything. Man, don't worry about the money. There will be plenty of money." Ben was on a roll now.

"I'm starting to like it. You don't know how much I hate this charter crap now."

"I know. You drag your butt in here every day with none of the fire you used to have. Before, you saw it as fishing and getting paid for it; now it's become babysitting a bunch of drunks. This will change all that. This is absolutely perfect. Perfect for you, perfect for Bulldog, perfect for the Rutherford Foundation, perfect for humanity, and perfect for the IRS."

"Put it together, Ben. I'm on board."

"Great. I've got to go. We're going fishing out by the North Ledge. The fridge is getting low on wahoo. After we fish, the boat's going back to Spanish Wells, so I won't see you because I'm leaving early in the morning. I'll call you tomorrow night, on Cora Lee's phone, not the single side band. Make it 8 o'clock."

"Ten roger. Y'all have fun. Tight lines to ya."

Bo closed the door behind him and locked it. He needed time to think. No, too much was happening too fast. He needed time to not think. Not even bothering to go to his bunk, he laid down on the salon floor exhausted. He noticed the book under the sofa. He had forgotten about it. Rolling over, he retrieved it. The hole through the middle was big enough to put his finger through, so he did. He spun that book on his finger and thought, we're all just islands in the stream; yeah Papa Hemingway, just islands in life's stream.

CHAPTER 29

Bo nursed U-Boat into second gear and headed up the Queen's Highway to find the dog. True to his word, he had made sure the mongrel had been fed and cared for. This evening was different. The pups were ready to go. He was sure the dog was ready for them to go. There were only three, but Bo figured there had to have been more; these were the strong ones. They weren't all that bad looking. Mongrel bred with mongrel can sometimes skip a few generations and come out all right; same with people. Bo had arranged homes for the three puppies.

Chris, Bo's favorite boat wash boy, wanted one, because a boy just needs a puppy. Swirly, the island's rasta man and chief voodoo practitioner, thought he could teach one to climb coconut trees and harvest the nuts. Bo figured Swirly was nuts, or his brand of voodoo must be mighty powerful. Swirly also grew the best weed on the island, so even if the dog couldn't climb trees, Swirly would swear he had seen him do it and be happy with his choice of canine. The Three Sisters wanted a puppy to guard the hen house. Bo had mentioned something about foxes guarding the hen house, but the sisters' concern was snakes. Anyway, the Three Sisters owned a small restaurant, so Bo knew the pup would eat well from table scraps.

The dog knew the sound of U-Boat and was waiting with her little family.

"Well, dog, tonight you finally get some relief. No peace for the weary, huh? I hope your tits suck up after these pups are gone and done sucking on them. Draggin' the ground like that's not gonna make me too proud. What the hell, everybody here thinks I'm crazy anyhow. Come on."

Bo threw them all in the back of the Jeep, wiggled the gear into first and cruised back down the highway. His first stop was Chris's house. The puppy was just what Chris needed, and Chris guaranteed three special boat washes in return. The next stop was the Three Sisters, and Bo picked up five free meals there. The final stop was Swirly's shack. Swirly was so appreciative he promised Bo a coconut and a joint.

He looked at his watch and saw it was already 8 o'clock. Ben would be calling. U-Boat skidded to a stop in the sand on the boat ramp, just as Cora Lee was calling for him.

"Bo, I've got great news," Ben's voice crackled over the phone. "The committee unanimously thought the idea was super, and they have agreed to fund the whole thing. Excuse the pun, but they bit hook, line, and sinker. I want to get started right away, so I'll use personal money right now, and the foundation will reimburse me later when they finish their paperwork and get organized."

"I appreciate it, Ben, but ..."

"First thing in the morning, I am wiring $500,000 to the Royal Bank of Canada. I am also faxing a Bill of Sale and stuff on the *Full Bloom* for you to sign. See Mr. Albury over there at the bank. You know him. He knows what to do. Pay off the boat and all its outstanding liabilities. The rest my friend, is all yours. Oh, by the way, I know the *Full Bloom* is the center of your life. Don't worry. This transaction will be for the accountants only. Everything will remain the same. It's only paper, Bo, only paper. If at any time this doesn't work out, the *Full Bloom* will be sold back to you for a dollar. Ten four?"

"Ben, man, I ... I don't know what to say."

"Say nothing. You earned it. Before long, a lot of people will owe you much more than this money can buy. I'll be down this weekend. See you." Click. Bo stood there with the phone in his hand, immobile.

"Bo, is there something wrong?" Cora Lee asked.

"No, Cora Lee, there is something right." He handed the phone to her and walked out. The dog had waited beside the door and followed and wagged behind him all the way down the dock.

"Bo! That's the ugliest damn dog I ever saw," someone yelled from the bar, accompanied by a lot of other laughter.

"Yeah, but look at those tits," he shot back. "Yeah, look at those tits. That's your name dog, Tits. Fits, Tits, don't it?"

Tits followed him to the boat, and took a place in the cockpit as if she had been there all her life. Bo went inside, still stunned from Ben's call, and pulled down another favorite classic, Neville Williams' *Sea Dogs*.

CHAPTER 30

"Darcy," Mrs. Webster called. "Here's a letter for you, Darcy."

"I'm in the kitchen, Momma."

Mrs. Webster came in and handed her a scuffed-up envelope with no return address. Darcy turned the knife she had been peeling potatoes with on the letter, and peeled it open without skipping a beat. She pulled out a check with *Full Bloom* printed in the upper left corner, and "your cut" scribbled in the lower left. It was for $50,000.

"Holy shit, Momma." The knife hit the floor. The check fluttered to the table. Mrs. Webster looked down, and then sat down.

"Darcy, you said he kept all that gold for himself."

"That's what I *thought*."

"But then you said his excuse was helping some kids, didn't you?"

"Yeah, that was his sorry excuse, I mean sorry, too."

"You know, maybe he did tell you the truth. I saw on the television a few weeks ago, I think it was the news, a story about a girl up in Atlanta that got a miracle. I remember she was dying from some awful disease, and this special gold was curing her."

"That's what he told me about. Momma, I wonder if he was really shooting straight with me?"

"I remember the disease was leukemia."

"That's what Atom's niece had. I can't believe this! He was telling the truth!" Damn you, Bo, you sonofabitch, she thought.

"Well, if he did give it away, where did this money come from?

And look how much it is!"

"I don't know where he got this money, but ... but, I don't know. I just know we're in the money now. I've never seen so much money."

"No, sweetheart. It's your money, not mine."

"You've been good to me, Momma, letting me run back here like a whipped dog with its tail between its legs. I'll take care of you. What goes around, comes around. Always. You took care of me when I came back. I know I was a pain in the rear end, mopin' around, not eating, bitchy."

"I knew you were hurt. Hurting bad. A mother knows these things. One day you will too."

"But, Momma, I didn't know *why* then. I know now. I thought I was hurt 'cause I lost out on all that gold. But you can't miss somethin' you never had. I know now. It was ... I missed Bo. I thought he lied to me. I thought he thought I was so dumb I'd believe that story. Just another guy thinking I was dumb. That's what hurt. I liked him, Momma, I really did. He was the only guy I ever met that could hold up to me. He was tough as me, Momma. The only guy tough as me. Bo was it, Momma. Now he's gone."

"Darcy, only your outside is tough. A mother knows these things."

"Momma, I have somewhere to go. Somewhere really important, to do something I've always dreamed about. I'll be back in a couple of hours."

Darcy ran out the back screen door with no shoes on, not even her flip-flops. She raced around the house, down Andrew Street, and up US 1, blowing open the big glass doors of the BMW dealership. A slicky salesman saw her coming.

"I want a red convertible, mister," she demanded.

"You came running in here to buy a car? Why not shoes first?"

"Why the fuck would I be in here if I didn't want to buy a car, asshole."

"Ah, yes, ma'am."

She was already headed for the show floor convertible. Her long legs sprung and she was in the convertible and behind the wheel, gripping it like she was already driving it at 100 miles per hour.

"It's nice, isn't it? Ma'am, did you see the sticker on this car?" It read $28,000.

"Change, buddy, change. That's what this is all about. *Change*."

The doors to the dealership opened again and an elegant, elderly lady, dripping in jewelry, walked in trailing a twenty-something guy behind her, decked out in designer clothes. The slicky salesman rushed and gushed toward her, thinking his chances were much better with them than with a girl with no shoes, who acted as if she was about to beat his ass.

"Now, Edward, if I buy you this 500 series, or whatever you call it, you have to hold to our promise."

"It's a 700 series, Mother, 700."

"Of course, dear. You are twenty-eight years old already, and have done nothing with your life. You have to promise to do something with your life. *Something*, Edward.

"I will, Mother. I will. Hey, look at this one."

"Edward. *Do something with your life*, Edward. Not I will, I will. I heard that when I bought you the condominium."

The words rang through Darcy's ears and echoed through her head. Do something with your life. Was this the wake-up bell, maybe an alarm?

She watched Edward and Mother and thought, here's a spoiled little brat that's had everything given to him. Money and the opportunity that money brings, and he's just a whiny little kid who can't and will never be able to say, "I did something and I did it by myself."

She got out of the car quietly, left the door hanging open, went to the literature rack, and grabbed the brochure with the color chart.

She left and no one noticed. She headed towards home, clutching the brochure. She would look at the car pictures with her Mom, and she would help her decide. Do something with your life. Damn, lady, why did you have to come in right then and say that shit? I was just fine before your rich ass walked in the door. Why couldn't you and your little piss-ant boy just go find his toy someplace else? DAMMIT!

She walked in the door of the pharmacy. Bare feet shuffled up to the rainbow colors of nail polish. She took bottle after bottle from the selection carousel, comparing the shade to the red color sample in the car literature. She found an exact match. She let the brochure slip to the floor and left it. Out the door and in the sunshine, she looked up at the sun and held her head back, trying not to let the tears fall, but her heart couldn't hold that much, and her eyes pooled up and flooded over anyway. Darcy, don't cry, she said to herself. Darcy's too tough to cry. Darcy, just don't cry. People passed and looked and the tears streamed and she didn't care.

Before she would have cared about not caring; be a tough ass and show it. But something had warmed over her like a religious revelation. Bo did it. Bo did the right thing. Your turn, Darcy. You can't make it come, but when it comes, you can't do anything about it either; that is the good thing. Well, she said to herself, at least I got the friggin' nail part of this deal.

Now! Now, go do something, Darcy. You can. You're not dumb. You're smart. You can. A chance of a lifetime in a lifetime of chances, Darcy. Grab it, Darcy. Go for it, Darcy. Good bye, Darcy. Hello, Darcy. Flip Flop.

CHAPTER 31

This was homecoming day for Bulldog. The whole island took the day off for the festivities. It was going to be a surprise party. Bo had gone to Nassau to collect him in the *Full Bloom* and give him a comfortable ride back. He let him lie on the sofa on the port side rather than in the center of the boat for balance, as was customary. That was special enough for Bulldog. He just couldn't believe Bo didn't make him lie in the middle on the floor. As Bo pulled up to the dock, he told Bulldog to stay put inside until things were secured. He didn't want Bulldog to see the what was going on outside.

Once docked, Bo helped Bulldog up with the aid of crutches made out of two by fours, Bo slung the salon door open, and Bulldog bounded out, looking down. Suddenly the crowd of children saw him. They couldn't hold it in: "Bulldog! Bulldog! Bulldog!" they all chanted. The dock was overloaded with hundreds of children and their mothers and fathers and uncles and aunts. Every kid on Briland was there to welcome Bulldog home.

The grin on his face was so broad that his massive cheeks came up and forced his eyes shut. The joy was in his ears: "Bulldog! Bulldog! Bulldog!" they kept chanting as they jostled and bumped him though the crowd to the fire wagon. He lost his crutches, but the giant couldn't fall because of the hundreds of kids pressed to his legs, supporting him.

The fire wagon had been prepared with a throne for the grand occasion. They sat Bulldog on the throne. The procession began down Bay Street, with the school marching band in tow. Children ran alongside, throwing candy at Bulldog. It was a real switch, because for so many years when Bulldog was Santa, he threw candy to them. He just basked in the glory, and that's just what they wanted him to do. This was Bulldog's own personal carnival, and the band played on behind him, out of rhythm, out of key, out of tune, with every one of the clarinets screeching.

Everybody on the island lined the street, cheering, dancing, joyful. The older women were waving colorful handkerchiefs and calling out, "God Bless You, boy! Praise de Lawd! You's a good boy, Bulldog! You come roun' my kitchen, I fix you up! We love you, Bulldog!"

They progressed up Bay Street, the whole crowd falling in behind, singing and praising. At the fig tree and the government dock they turned up the hill on Governor's Road. The cottages were as blue as the day's sky and as bright as the sky's sun, and the bougainvillea was redder than the fire wagon. Around the whole town of Dunmore, they carried on until they arrived at Bulldog's little house. The men had painted it bright Bahamian blue; the girls had scrubbed the inside; the women had loaded it with every kind of imaginable island food; and the kids had trimmed the yard. They helped him down and into the house, and put him in his bed. Groups had been scheduled for care watches, and they took their posts.

Bo went in to check. Bulldog's eyes were closed now from the puffiness of crying. Bo had never seen the big man cry. He was tired from the ride back and from the emotional festivities and the pain pills, prescribed by the triple dose because of his size.

"You okay, big buddy?"

Bulldog just smiled his grin.

"I've got something for you." Bo reached in his pocket, pulled out a check, and held it in front of Bulldog's face.

"What is it, Boss? I cain't see it. A new lure?"

"No, Bull, it's a check for fifty thousand. For you."

"Yeah, Boss. These must be some good pills."

"Its real, Bull, and it's all yours. You earned it."

"Boss, that cain't be. I never done nothing to earn that kind of money."

"Yes, you did."

"Damn, Boss, with that kind of money I could be the real Santa now. Christmas for all the kids on Briland, even North Eleuthera, too, and for a long time, too. I cain't believe it. I cain't wait for Christmas, Boss. I gonna be Santa now, right, Boss, ten roger?"

"Ten roger, Bull. To a lot of kids you were always Santa, Bull. Their only Santa."

The pain pills now had taken over. Bo folded the check into that huge catcher's mitt of a hand, and Santa sighed and fell asleep. Bo was sure there were sugar plums dancing in his head. On the way out, Bo overheard the two elderly ladies fussing about the place, just because fussing was what they did best.

"Bulldog's home."

"Santa's home."

"Praise de Lawd."

CHAPTER 32

Bo jumped in U-Boat with Tits sitting proudly beside him and headed up to the north end and Ward's house. Bo walked in the pool house; Ward was kicked back by the pool.

"Hey, Ward. How you doin'?"

"Great, Bo. That sure was some welcoming party for Bulldog."

"Man, I'll tell you. If we could be loved just a tenth of how they love him."

"We don't deserve it a tenth as much as he does, Bo."

"I know I sure as shit don't. Well, congratulations on winning the Bahamas Billfish Championship with the new boat."

"That was a hell of a fish, Bo. We fought her for four hours. And you know we didn't even hook up until ten minutes before lines in. I guess your little magic transmission fluid did the trick."

"It was a lucky guess, Ward. I've got something for you." Bo whipped a folded check out of his back pocket. It was for $25,000, plus twenty percent interest calculated to the day, to the penny.

"No way, Bo. We had a deal about the boat."

"That was your deal, Ward, not mine," Bo said, pushing the check toward him.

"Okay." He took the check.

"I've talked to Ben about the research center. It sounds like a great idea. Hell, it gets you into the thing you love, but in a different and much better way. I want to help." Ward took a pen from the bar and endorsed the back of the check and handed it to Bo.

"My first contribution to the research center."

Bo took the check back.

"Damn you, Ward."

Ward smiled and said, " C'mon, Captain, let's have a beer."

CHAPTER 33

The Rutherford Foundation had placed another $500,000 in the bank for the construction of the research facility. Bo was busy with a ton of things. The center had to be designed. Architectural drawings, engineering drawings, land planning drawings, power distribution, and docks all had to be developed. Once the designs were completed, they had to be submitted to the proper authorities in Nassau for approvals. Everything was slow, or at least it couldn't move fast enough for Bo. He was in Nassau half the time and couldn't fish at all. He needed Bulldog anyway.

Bulldog was getting better fast. In only three weeks, he was walking himself to Willie's and shooting pool, harvesting the tourists' dollars more out of habit than need. He still wrestled with the belief that he had all that money now. By the fifth week Bulldog was good to go.

Bo had tormented, abused, and generally pissed off every authority in Nassau, and decided he better get out of town before they ran him off. His architect could handle Nassau a little more diplomatically. Back on Harbour Island, Bo and Bulldog started fishing again, and it felt good. The Mother Ocean was their element, not some stuffy bureaucrat's offices in the city.

The original two nuggets Bo had sent Atom yielded 50 charms. Those had been distributed through Dr. Jane Daniel. The recovery rate of the children was astonishing. It was not short of a miracle. Julia, who had her charm first and therefore the longest, was in total remission. In only three months, she had escaped the clutches of a tragic death and was, by all appearances, healthy. Atom and Jane had not yet figured it out, but they were arriving at some logical possibilities.

The press naturally picked up on it, and the gold became the cover story of several national magazines. The Mayo Clinic joined in with research studies and Emory University School of Medicine was searching for other applications. Atom ended up being hounded by the press for answers, but he wouldn't reveal the source of the "mystery metal." That was the pact he had made with Bo. Bo jokingly suggested to Atom that maybe he should just tell them the truth, because there was no way they would believe a crazy story like that anyway.

Atom requested a sample of the water from as far down as Bo could get it. Bulldog and Bo had rigged a double wire contraption to a container and secured a sample from 2,000 feet. When Atom analyzed the water, he found significant quantities of molecular gold. That molecular gold had the same atomic structure as the nuggets. Atom was sure the source was the fissures spewing minerals up from the bottom. Bulldog said the earth was "throwin' up."

The theory that Atom constructed, and was very confident about, was reasonable. Every time these fish washed water over their gills to breathe, the molecular gold would enter into their bloodstream. For some reason these fish would filter the gold out of the bloodstream and collect it in a cyst in their gullet. The cyst was some non-essential membrane left over from ancient times, just as the human appendix is today. Atom also explained it was kind of like the filter system of the kidneys.

By taking into account the size of the fish Bo was catching, the size of their gills and the estimated age of the fish, Atom had even figured each fish would have washed 19,710,000 gallons of the gold-enriched water over its gills. Matching that to the concentration of the gold in the sample yielded a remarkably accurate prediction of the nugget size. As the deposit grew, the fish developed that tough sinewy pouch to protect itself from the foreign material.

Bo understood that. He figured it was like how pearls grow to protect the clam from the foreign sand. Atom's other theory was the fish needed some nutrient in the water that was particular *only* to the fissures. They needed this nutrient to live, so they stayed right there in that one place, enabling them to consume that much gold over their lifetimes. There was still the question of the extraordinary atomic weight. Atom would substantiate his theories, eventually. As Atom always said, the numbers don't lie. It always worked out neatly.

The gold was shipped weekly to Atom, who had arranged for an Atlanta lab to process and mint it. They had decided all the charms would be in the shape of starfish. The box each charm was sent in was the azure color of the Bahamian waters and was engraved on the top in gold with the inscription, *When You Wish Upon A Star*. The nuggets were averaging 25 charms each. In the past four months, Bo had shipped enough for 3,200 charms. That was 3,200 children helped. It even made hard-ass Bo feel good.

CHAPTER 34

In the fifth month, he received all the plans from Nassau stamped <u>Approved</u>. Bo went about hiring local contractors to build the facility and the dock system. The estimated time was four months, which Bo knew would be at least eight. Every day he rode herd over the contractors and at night fished for the gold.

He didn't have time to search the beach during the day, or the bars at night, for companionship. He didn't want to. He was just not interested anymore. He didn't need a night or two of brief temporary laughter, drinks, dancing on the beach, and un-loving sex. Leave all that to Romero. He had done good; he had done what was right, and he had done it right, and he was proud. All he wanted was to share it with somebody. Somebody. He had accomplished a lot, he had grown a lot, and all he wanted to hear was, "You done good, Bo, you did the right thing, Bo. I'm proud of you, Bo." But he also wished that somebody would be his lover, too. He needed a partner, a partner in life. But nobody was in sight.

Just as Bo had predicted, the center was receiving the last touches at the end of eight months, not four. Bo was sitting at a desk in the lab, scratching out some numbers. It had been a year and four months since the very first gold fish. To date, he and Bulldog had caught and shipped enough gold for 10,000 charms.

He kicked back, put his hands behind his head, his bare feet up on the table, and closed his eyes. That night rolled around in his head; that *first* fish. The surprise, the frantic mutilation, looking for more, the nude wash-down party, and the rum were all as clear in his memory as the Bahamian waters.

But so much has happened. Darcy. Where was Darcy? That dumb broad was probably in some bar conducting herself as a "professional server, you know." Yeah, I know, peas or corn; whiskey, now Twinkies, what the shit? Those flip-flops, *man*, how dumb can you get? The very day she got that check she probably spent every dime on a red BMW convertible. But she had made him feel alive. Where was she living now?

She was something. She had a fire about her. Deep down, he liked her, liked her a lot. She was the only woman he had ever respected. Respected. Why? He didn't know why. He *did* know. He did. She had been a partner. It had hurt when she left.

"Boss!" Bulldog rang out, coming around the corner.

"In here, Bull," he called as he dropped his feet to the floor.

"Where you been?"

"Over in Spanish Wells, Boss."

"What the hell you been doing over there? For months now you been going at least every other day."

"I'm gonna show you." He reached behind and around the corner. "Meet Cassie, Bo."

Shyly, a girl of about twenty appeared. She had short-cropped blond hair, enormous green eyes, a dimpled smile and was all of ninety pounds.

"We're gettin' married!" Bulldog blurted out, unable to contain himself.

"I'll be damned," Bo whispered in shock. Bulldog had never shown any interest in girls. Bo figured he just didn't have the confidence to try because of his weight.

"Well, congratulations," Bo said. "When?"

"Right after New Year's. Ain't she great?" He was grinning like Bo had never seen before. A man in love.

"Bull, any girl good enough for you has to be great."

"We had to tell you first, Boss, but now we gotta go. I'm gonna show her off to the whole island." He picked her up and threw her on his shoulders, her little legs straddling his neck and draping down like a too-short scarf. Bulldog paraded out, bouncing her on his massive shoulders.

Bo sat a while. Stunned. He put his head in his hands. Bulldog has got a girl. He was happy for him. He was a good man and deserved it. That girl would be waited on hand and foot by the gentle giant. She got the best part of the deal. In his own loneliness and with mixed feelings of joy for Bulldog and frustration at his own solitude, he let his head drop to the table and crashed the corner of his eye right into the razor sharp edge of a conch shell.

"Shit! Damn!" he grabbed his head as the blood gushed down the side of his face. Throwing some ice in a rag, he went outside, jumped into the golf cart, and headed for the clinic to get sewn up, again.

CHAPTER 35

The palm fronds were shuffling and rustling as Bo screeched the golf cart to a stop in front of the clinic. In his hurry, he didn't lock the parking brake when he slid out, and the cart rolled down the hill a few yards, until it was stopped by a concrete block wall. Bo didn't look back and neither did the 20 school children waiting outside. They were more interested in the bloody rag Bo was holding to the side of his head. Runaway carts were common, but that much blood was not. They peeled out of the way as Bo passed.

"Cap'n Bo', you awright?"

"Cap'n Bo', wha happen?"

"Mon, look at dat blood."

"I'm fine, kids, just a cut, that's all. Miss Melanie will fix it up. Don't you worry."

The old linoleum tile was gritty on his bare feet. He rattled the yellow porcelain knob on the door bearing a hand-written sign stating, Do Not Enter Until Called. He figured his ticket was his bloody rag. He'd been sewn up here before, many times. The room was light lime green and trimmed in white that had gone gray over the years. A big metal desk stacked high with papers and charts occupied the middle of the room. Little patient tables, little in that none of them could hold the full length of an adult body, hugged the perimeter walls. Only the file cabinets between them served as privacy curtains. Bo figured pulling out the drawers could help, but not much.

The assistant, Esther, looked up and without the first hint of concern or surprise, said, "Goes on in dare, Cap'n Bo, I gets Miss Melanie," as she nodded to an adjacent little room with a door.

Miss Melanie took care of the entire island. She was a black Bahamian, about half Bulldog's size, with skin as smooth and clear as that of a moray eel. Her mouth was as full of teeth as a moray's, too, big bright white ones which gave her a glorious smile that was warm and comforting, unlike a moray eel's.

"Let's see here, Mr. Bo," Miss Melanie said as she pulled the rag sodden with melting ice and blood away from Bo's face.

"Good cut, but clean. Won't be much of a scar."

"But, Miss Melanie, I want a scar. That's me."

"You gots plenty, Mr. Bo. Awright, let's get it clean. You won't need a tetanus shot. I gave you one just nine months ago. Turn your head to the wall and be still."

Bo did what he was told as he heard the tearing and the peeling apart of cleaning packages and disposable suture kits. Miss Melanie dabbed and patted; then she shot the area with a deadening medication from a tiny syringe. She placed a disposable paper cover over his entire face. The cover had a hole in it that she centered over the wound and his eye. Miss Melanie began to stitch.

All Bo could see through a little corner of the cover was the big poster plastered on the wall, concerning and warning all about venereal disease. The only part of it that he could see was the column on vaginal discharge. To take his mind off the work Miss Melanie was doing, he read it all. Thirty minutes later, he had read it three times over and couldn't believe there were so many types of vaginal discharges. It made him glad he didn't have a vagina. It also worried him.

"What the hell did you do?" Ben's voiced boomed in.

"How'd you know I was here?" Bo answered.

"Followed the blood."

"You want to wait till I get this haircut done, or you want to talk now?"

"Let's talk now. I'm going fishing in an hour."

"That's fine. Miss Melanie, here, isn't gonna let me move, so you have a hooked audience."

"Bo, you know how stuffy those assholes on the board of directors are?"

"Watch you mouth in my clinic, boy."

"Yes, ma'am. I'm sorry. They like the work you are doing down here, but and, it's an arrogant but, they feel the place needs some more academic credibility. They want to hire a degree'd person to run it. You know these kinds of boards are usually filled with Ph.D.s, which in my mind means, Piled Higher and Deeper."

"Dat's da truth. I seen and know more than most of dem doctors," agreed Miss Melanie.

"They just can't believe someone without a ten-page 'curriculum vitae' could know anything or do anything. They've been on my ass - oh, I'm sorry, Miss Melanie. They've been on my case to get someone in the center with some academic credentials."

Melanie was humming as she stitched. Ben found a metal folding chair and dragged it up backwards to sit.

"Ben, I've got little respect for those academic airheads. They're usually just smart asses, not smart."

"Bo, you gonna get a shot in you bottom if you don't watch dat mouth."

"Yes, ma'am, Miss Melanie."

"I know. I know. I at least convinced them to let me do the placement search. That way I can get someone in here you can probably live with."

"I doubt that, Ben. Who do you know that knows that ocean like me and Bull? Who do you know who has the feel, and can tell the feel, of even the texture of the water? I don't need some school kid coming in here telling me what to do, or how to do it."

"Calm down, Bo, or you will have that scar," Miss Melanie said.

"That's right. Calm down, Bo. Don't worry. I'll find someone good. It's just figurehead stuff anyway, and I'll be sure they know it."

"How soon?"

"They want someone in here the first of January to match the funding for the next year."

"It's Thanksgiving in a few days. That's quick. Do what you gotta do, Ben, but you better get someone tough, cause I'm gonna bust their academic ass. Ow! Shit!" Bo felt what had to be a horse needle go right through his shorts and right in his rear end.

"I gonna take dis suture and sew you mouth shut, boy."

"I like your spunk, Miss Melanie," Ben said. "How long have you run this clinic?"

"Ten long years. It's tough to make da ends come together when most of it I give away for free."

Ben was looking around. "Why are all those school children out there?" he asked.

"Dey here for dey shots."

"Free?"

"Yeah. Some pay me with fruits and vegetables, an' some pay with helping out, howsever dey can."

"How much for stitching up Bo?"

"He be fifty dollas. It's all fifty dollas no matter what, no matter how long."

"Well, Miss Melanie, I'll cover Bo, since he got cut on the job."

Ben was pulling out his checkbook. "Who do I make it out to?"

"Princess Margaret Clinic."

"Thanks, Ben. Tight lines to ya," Bo said.

"All right, I gotta go catch a tuna. I'll see you later, Bo."

On his way out Ben dropped a check for $50,000 on that big metal desk. That came to $5,000 a stitch.

The phone was ringing when Bo pulled back in to the center.

Bo had to move quicker than he wanted to, to catch it. The hurrying made his head throb.

"Bo!" Atom's voice came through.

"Hey, Atom. How are you?"

"Great, just great. Jane and I are getting closer. We've got some potentially credible theories that are fleshing out. It's been 16-hour days, side by side, working this out, but we're close, real close. And here's the other good news - Jane and I are getting closer in other ways, too. We're getting engaged."

"WHAT!"

"That's right. I never, never, thought I'd find anybody intellectually stimulating enough for me, except for Bulldog, but there she was all along. Isn't that great?"

"That *is* great, Atom. Great!"

"We're staying here for Christmas and New Year's to be with her folks, but right after that we're coming down. We're even bringing Julia. Get us a room at Runaway Hill, if you can. I'll talk to you later. Have a great Christmas, Bo. Bye."

Stunned for the second time in as many hours, with a sliced head to boot, Bo leaned against the wall. Bo had *never* even imagined his two best friends finding partners. Shit! He went for the rum bottle and started gulping. What about him? Where was his better class of bimbos? Where was his side cover? Shit! Why was he all alone and lonely?

He gulped the rum with purpose and vengeance. In thirty minutes the fresh quart was gone. The bottle crashed and shattered on the concrete wall, not because he had no use for it anymore, but because he had no use for himself anymore. He wobbled to the cot in the corner and lay down. The old man from the sea flashed through his head for a fleeting second before he passed out. Was he going to turn out to be *him*?

CHAPTER 36

Bo woke to bright sunshine. The cut was stinging and his head was throbbing. He downed a handful of aspirin with a new bottle of rum. Twenty minutes later, U-Boat skidded on the sand at Cash's Liquor Store, almost throwing Tits out. Armed with a case of rum and a case of orange juice, he worked U-Boat up to the north end.

Tits knew something wasn't right. She tried to lick his face, and he hurled her out into the brush yelling, "Go the fuck back to where your mangy ass came from. Bitch!"

Fifty yards later, he locked the wheels and spun in reverse. Tits jumped back in. She knew he needed her, and she owed him a lot. She was his now, no matter how he treated her.

"Come on, dammit. You're probably the best bitch I'm ever gonna get."

At a small turn-off, he gunned the jeep through the thick brush and up the hill. At the top there was a clearing with a small lean-to shack. Swirly had made the shelter years ago to have a place to practice voodoo and smoke weed. Driftwood made up the only two walls that supported a thatch roof. This was a special place. It was the highest point on the island, and overlooked the dazzling color of the Mother Ocean. Below were the dark splotches of living coral heads, separated by turquoise. Waves broke white foam over some of the highest, then sizzled into silence, waiting for the next one. On and on and on.

Bo settled onto the straw with Tits obediently beside him and drank, alternating a swig of rum and a gulp of juice. He looked out far, and just stared. He watched the Mother Ocean like a widow watching for a ship that never comes in. Waiting. Like the widow.

For two days he drank, pissed, passed out, and waited.

Bulldog was worried. He didn't know what happened or where Bo was. He asked everybody, and as he did, the worry spread. Finally, he ran into Swirly.

"Does know no ting bout da matter," Swirly said as he toked on a joint.

"I'm real scared, Swirly. We've got to find him. Help me," Bulldog said, turning to leave but wandering in circles not knowing what to do or where to look next.

"Waits. Has you go round my voodoo to-lean, ups da top?"

"No."

"Go there. He's there. I feels it. Best you goes by youself. Only take *care* wit you. I feels a wounded animal holed up in de brush. Dat animal needing of time to lick of his wounds."

Bulldog took off. Swirly took another toke.

Elephants can't move through brush quietly; neither does a Bulldog. Bo knew it was Bulldog from the sound. He laid back on his elbows and waited. Bulldog saw U Boat and smiled a cautious relief. When he finally made it to the top, he stood over an unshaven, dirty Bo, smelling of sweat, rum, and urine.

"Boss, you don't look so good."

"I don't feel worth a shit either. In fact I'm not worth a shit."

"What's wrong, Boss?"

"You wouldn't fuckin' understand, Bull."

"Let me help you home."

"No way. Where the hell is home, anyway?"

"Boss, you need help an I'm the best help you can get."

"Don't worry about my ass, Bull. I'm a big boy."

"Boss, you the biggest man I ever known. You, *Cap'n Bo.* Sometimes we all need help though, Boss."

"You can't help me, Bull. Only a good woman can help me and that ain't in the cards. Tits here just don't cut it."

"It can happen, Boss. Look, it happened to me. To me, Boss, a quarter-ton dumb ass. If it can happen for me, it damn sure can happen for you. Please, Boss."

"Bull, thanks, but get your ass out of here."

"Boss, you think I don't understand cause I'm not as smart as you, but I do. All them years, I seen you go through so many beautiful girls while I just shot pool."

"You're full of shit. I was a perfect gentleman to every damn one of them."

"No, Boss. You were a gentleman to get what you wanted. *Get*, Boss, not *give*. The only person you ever gave to was me and you know what? I'm the only person here now. The only one you gave to is the only one here. Look around you. What else you see?"

"The Mother Ocean, that's all. That's all."

"No, Boss, look beside you, right there."

"Tits?"

"Yeah, Boss, Tits. Tits is the only other thing besides me you gave to. The only two and we're here. Don't it make sense, Boss? Wait. You gave to Darcy, too, but two out of three ain't bad, is it Boss?"

"Darcy. Two out of three ain't bad. Roll your fat ass out of here."

"I will, Boss, but I'll be back in the morning, and there ain't nothing you can do about it. Just like you promised Tits. I'll be back. Night, Boss."

———•———

The next morning Bulldog brought a plate of Ma Ruby's French toast and bacon. He set it beside Bo and walked away. Neither one of them said a word. In fact, neither one of them even looked at each other. Bulldog was worried, though. He huddled in town with

Uncle Ulmer, Beulah, Swirly, Ma Ruby and the Three Sisters.

"You just cain't go up there an git him," Ma Ruby said.

"Dat boy tough. He can whip any bodies in dese Bahamas, 'cept maybe you, Bulldog," one of the Three Sisters noted.

"He come down, when he ready. I told you, he be a wounded animal," Swirly warned.

"I got to do somethin'," Bulldog pleaded.

Bo had been on the hill for four days, drinking. Tomorrow was Thanksgiving. Bahamians don't celebrate it, but there are so many Americans in the Bahamas that Ma Ruby had fixed the traditional turkey, dressing, sweet potatoes and even a pumpkin pie. Bulldog trudged himself and the turkey dinner up the hill. He placed it down on Bo's lap. By now, Bo's eyes had glazed over and he seemed to be in a trance. Bulldog didn't like the looks of it.

"Boss, I'm taking you home. Home to the *Full Bloom*, where you belong."

Nothing. Just staring out at the Mother Ocean, like the widow. Bulldog reached down to help him up. When he did, Bo kicked him hard, right in the gut. The plate scattered. The gut's not where you kick Bulldog; it has no effect other than to hurt his feelings. Bulldog acted like he was going to fix the plate back up. When he picked up that big drumstick, he slammed it across Bo's head so hard that slivers of meat flew off for ten yards. Bo fell on his back, out cold turkey. Bulldog threw him over his shoulder and carried him the two miles back to the boat. Tits followed with the bone in her mouth. Bulldog put him to bed where he belonged.

"Here, Boss." Bulldog took the turkey wishbone out of his shirt pocket and put it in Bo's hand. He held Bo's hand with his and pulled the other side with his other hand. The wishbone broke in Bulldog's favor. He won; he grinned. His wish was for his friend.

CHAPTER 37

Uncle Ulmer, Swirly, Beulah, and the Three Sisters all convened in the back room next to the kitchen of the Three Sisters eatery.

"Awright. We uns got to save Bo."

"Amen. Amen."

"Bo gots to have a girl."

"Nots a girl. A real *woman*."

"Dats right. Amen."

"We gots to do our bestest voodoo now. What's da mix, ladies?"

"Well, we gots to have a doll. An we peerin' for love, so we gots to have love."

"Amen. I tink we gots to have da Mother Ocean water. Dat Mother Ocean, it be runnin' through Bo. It be in da boy's veins."

"Dat's right on. An, blood. Ain't voodoo with no blood."

"Amen. Amen. Chicken blood won't do. We cain't hook Bo up with no chicken."

"Well, we is lookin' for a chick, sorts kinda."

"Dats exactly de problem. All Bo gets and gots is dose chicks. He needs a woman, not chicks."

"Amen. Amen."

"We needs Bo's blood."

"Bulldog say he done cut hissef."

"Yeah. Dat was four days back. Dat cut done flaked over. We needs da fresh blood."

"You cain't just go an cut da boy ."

"No. No. Remember for you go down on da schooner, we sprinkle dem sharp tacks all on de deck so anybodies come on de boat, dem tacks stick in dey feets and dey yelp an yelp 'til dey jumps back to da water."

"Dats right. Dem tacks. Amen."

"Awright. I gets da blood. Beulah, we cain't use da regular dolls. Dis is special. We needs special."

"I knows, an I been ponderin'. Ponderin' mighty hard, an I got an idear. I gets da doll. Nots to fret. I gets da doll."

"Three Sistahs, yous gets da water. Midnight water too. Gots to be da midnight Mother Ocean water. Gets some pink sand too."

"Amen. Amen. Amen."

"What we gonna do bout da love? How we get love? We always voodooin' hate an dats easy with da sticks an dem pins. But love, whats we gonna do bout dat?"

"Dat is a fresh one. No doubt bout it. No doubt."

"Ain't it curious. We can come up with de hate so easy. Everbody can come up with de hate so easy, easy as Ulmer can fall down. But dat love, we just cain't deliver dat up. Hates easy; loves hard."

"Truth in dat, sister. Truth in dat indeedy."

"I gots an idear on dat. I bring somethin close. Close now, not da real ting. Da real ting a body just cain't own. Love cain't be owned, gots to be given."

"Amen, brother. Amen."

"Everbody gots dey 'structions? Awright, awright. Morrow night brings you tings an we commence to gets Bo a real woman."

———•———

That morning Swirly sent Chris down to the dock with the message that he needed to see Bo. Bo was up. He had raided the aspirin bottle but downed them with juice instead of rum. A three, four, five day binge, hell, he didn't know. He knew he felt good to be home, back on the *Full Bloom*, even though he didn't know how he got there. Well, he said to himself, I'm not happy. I'm lonely but I can't just quit. I've never quit any damn thing in my life. I'm the toughest sonofabitch I know.

"What the hell does Swirly want, Chris?" he yelled out the door.

"I doesn't know, Cap'n Bo."

"Life goes on doesn't it? I guess I'll go see what he wants," he muttered.

"Yessir, Cap'n Bo."

Bo arrived at Swirly's and knocked on the screen door. It fell off its hinges and into the bushes. Swirly came, saw the door, said nothing. Bo said nothing. It was like it didn't happen and who cared and so what? Bahamas.

"Bo, my mon. Come on in de house. Wanna beer?"

"Yeah, a real cold one. What do you want?"

Swirly fetched some ice-cold beers and threw the caps on the floor. They sat on some lawn furniture, inside. A two-ton, 20-year old console TV also sat in the corner, lopsided because two of the legs had poked holes and fallen through the rotten floor.

"Bo, I gots an idear. It's about shoes. Shoes to put on when you on de boat. You know all dem little suckers on face side on de starfish? Dem suckers can grab you leg like a boy puppy dog. Ifin you was to put dem suckers onto the bottoms side of de shoes, you stays put on de deck when de big wave comes. Right?"

"Swirly, those suckers have to be alive to do what they do."

"Gimme you shoes there, Bo. I show you."

Bo slipped out of his shoes and kicked them towards Swirly. Swirly picked the shoes and himself up and headed for the side room.

"Come in here, Bo. I show you."

Bo followed. Three steps later, "God damn! Shit! What the hell!" Bo fell backward on his butt holding both feet and examining the bottoms trying to determine what had happened.

"Oh mon, Bo! I's so sorry. I spilt dem tacks last week an forgetted to get dem up. I's so sorry." Swirly came to his aid with a ready rag.

"Just lay back. I fix dis."

Bo laid back and Swirly slowly picked razor sharp tacks out of the soles of Bo's feet. As he did he squeezed each puncture to bleed it as much as possible, and wiped and collected the blood. When he was done the rag was more red than white. Swirly had gotten Bo's blood. He put Bo's shoes back on him when he was finished and helped him up.

"I guess you right about dem suckers, Bo. I knowed I can count on you fancy head for all de answers. I's real sorry bout dem tacks."

Bo headed for the door, as if he were walking on eggshells. What the hell is happening to me? He wondered. Is this real, or have I got so much rum in my body my liver's swapped places with my brain?

"I gotta go."

"Tanks for da blood."

"What?"

Swirly just smiled, showing weed smoke stained teeth.

———◆———

That night the voodoo clan congregated. Swirly had the bloody rag. Uncle Ulmer produced one of his passion flowers. The Three Sisters had a mayonnaise jar of midnight Mother Ocean water and a plastic beach bucket full of pink sand. Beulah pulled a naked Barbie doll from a paper bag. Things were coming together.

"Dey sure do put a figgur on dem dolls."

"Yeah, dat'll get Bo."

"Awrights, let's commence."

"Swirly, puts dat blood rag in da jar, an let it soak dat blood into da Mother Ocean. Beulah, hands me dat doll. Sistah Two, gets me one of you knit needles."

Sister Two came back with a needle, and Ulmer pulled a match from his pocket, lit it, and heated the end of the needle. With the hot, sharp point he burned a hole right in the center of Barbie's chest. Then he took the passion flower and inserted the stem into the hole.

"See. De passion flower goes deep side her to her heart. Sistah One, gets me dat sand."

Uncle Ulmer dug Barbie's pointed feet into the bucket of sand until she could stand on her own.

"Sistah Three, shake dat jar. We needs to leach all dat blood into da Mother Ocean."

Sister Three began shaking and dancing around the room chanting. The water was turning pink. Beulah was lighting candles. Swirly got a barstool and put it in the middle of the room, and on the stool Ulmer placed the bucket with the naked Barbie. They all sat on the floor looking up to the shrine they had built. Uncle Ulmer delivered the request to the voodoo gods.

"We uns here is you faithful. We uns here don aks no ting for us uns. Bo been sittin' too long on dat barstool. Bo done fall off dat barstool, too, but he just gets right back on. Bo needs to trade dat barstool for dat girl we faithful done placed on top off it."

Ulmer opened the mayonnaise jar and dipping with a chicken feather drew drops of the pink liquid and then let the drops fall to the center of the passion flower.

"Dis is da Mother Ocean. An in dat Mother Ocean be Bo's blood. With dat potion we faithful put into da passion flower, and through da flower into da heart of dat girl. Bo blood, and Mother Ocean, true passion, to the heart. Bo needs her heart."

They all took turns dropping the pink potion into the flower and began chanting and moaning and rocking. It went on for hours until all of the Bo blood and Mother Ocean was just a puddle on the floor. Finally, their trance state exhausted them, and they fell on the floor and slept.

The voodoo had been done, and nothing could exorcise what had been set in motion.

CHAPTER 38

"Dr. Campbell. Ben Rutherford here. How have you been?"

"Fine, Ben. You?"

"Fine too, Bill."

Dr. Bill Campbell headed up the prestigious Oceanographic School at the University of Miami.

"You've heard about our new research center over on Harbour Island, haven't you?" Ben asked.

"Sure have. Heard some good things, too."

"Well, the board of trustees up in New York wants me to find someone with some academic credentials to be the director. There's one problem, though. The guy running it now is the best sportfisherman in the business. He's tough and he knows the ocean."

"Is that the legendary Cap'n Bo? He has a reputation damn near as long as the Key West road."

"Yeah, that's what I'm dealing with. It's going to be hard to find someone compatible. I need someone that will work with him. The fact that this person is going to be called the 'director' is just to please the board. Whoever we choose will really be working for Bo. Have you got anybody in the school that might want something like that?"

"Matter of fact, I think I do."

"Now realize, I don't want an academic type, I want the academic paper. Hands on, Bill, a hands-on type."

"I've got a candidate. This person has been taking a triple load for a year. I've never had a student like this, maybe one of the sharpest I've ever taught ... not maybe, I'm sure."

"Credentials?"

"Not yet, but with correspondence and field work over there, it won't be a problem. This student is totally determined and the hardest worker I've ever had here. Oh, by the way, this candidate set up a program to teach underprivileged kids about marine life, even after all the work in the institute. Everybody in Miami is raving about it. Contributions have been flooding in. Maybe some field trips to the Bahamas could be arranged for these kids. It's quite a program."

"But, Bill. I need credentials."

"Don't worry about it, Ben. You tell your board to call me."

"If that's your first choice, I'm sure they will go along. Next problem. I need someone there January first."

"Well, the quarter is over in two weeks for Christmas, so it should work. Give me a few days to talk it over and I'll get back to you."

"Thanks for coming through, Bill."

"No problem. This one can handle your Cap'n Bo."

CHAPTER 39

For the month of December, Bo holed up in the lab during the day. He and Bulldog fished at night. There wasn't the usual joking and carrying on. It was kind of like ... just business. Bo was sullen, not moody, just didn't say much. Bulldog was worried, but stayed out of his way. Every night when they came in, they both did their respective chores. Bulldog would simply say "good night." After he left, Bo would go for the bottle and sleep with it.

A week before Christmas, Bulldog chartered a plane to Ft. Lauderdale. Santa was in the workshop. Santa Bulldog went to Toys R Us. He had the time of his life. It took three full days for him to hand pick more than 500 toys. He could have done the job quicker, but he had to play with each one of them first. After the first three shopping carts full, the store management became suspicious of this giant in shorts, old T-shirt, and worn deck shoes. When they questioned him, he pulled out a wad of hundreds and started peeling them off. The store manager examined a few of them for counterfeit. Once he was satisfied they were real, Bulldog had a special representative assigned to him.

Bulldog was a special customer; he was Santa. He would pick, play, approve, and the representative would have them wrapped and piled in a truck. Bulldog had never had so much fun. A larger plane had to be chartered just to carry it all, and Bulldog, back to Briland.

When he landed, Mr. Cooper, the customs official, was astonished, as cart after cart of presents came out of the plane. The last thing out was Bulldog.

"Hi, Mr. Cooper."

"Hi, Bulldog. You go shopping?"

"Yes sir. I sure did," Bulldog said, just beaming.

"How much did you spend, so I can figure the duty."

"$7,462.18."

Mr. Cooper wrote that figure down on his pad; then started scratching the math.

"Well, my figures show $2.14. I'll cover it. Merry Christmas, Bulldog."

"Put the word out for me, will ya? All the kids, Christmas Eve day, noon, the Fig Tree. Okay?"

"You got it, Santa."

———————•———————

On Christmas Eve day, at noon, the island's fire truck rolled down Bay Street with Santa Bulldog sitting atop of it, surrounded by all those presents. A tinny sounding cassette player blared all it could blare, "Jingle Bells." The children had been gathering around the fig tree since dawn. They came by boatloads from Spanish Wells, Governors Harbour, and all of North Eleuthera. All the Briland kids were there too.

Bulldog looked more like Santa than Santa himself. He was waving and throwing candy left and right and over his shoulder. The fire truck eased up under the fig tree, splendid with the ever present Christmas lights. Special steps were put in place so the children could climb up the back of the truck, receive their presents from Santa, and get down on another set of steps placed on the other side. It was factory line efficiency.

One by one, they filed up. Even though there were so many children, Bulldog made each one feel special. As they got to him, he would hug them, telling each child he or she was special, and then rummage around through the pile searching, finding for each one just that special present. It was dark before the truck was empty, but Bulldog was full.

Still in his Santa suit, Bulldog and Cassie knocked on the side of *Full Bloom*. Bo had been holed up drinking and peered at them blurry eyed.

"Merry Christmas, Boss. Cassie and me got a little something for you," he said, as he handed him the same azure box the charms were shipped in.

"Thank you, Bull. I'm sorry I didn't get you anything."

"You got me the best Christmas I ever had, Boss. Open it."

Bo wiggled the lid off the little box and reached in to pull out a belt buckle emblazoned with a perfect replica of the gold fish. He held it to the light and the gold glowed warm

"Where did you get this?" Bo said, as he admired it.

"I had Atom make it in Atlanta. He's the only other one who knows what those fish look like. It's our gold, Boss. I mean, our *special* gold. I figured, if that gold can do for those sick children the miracles they say, you might need a little yourself. They sure are a lot worse off than you."

Bo knew exactly what he meant. Bo threaded his old buckle off and put the new one on.

"Thank you, Bull. It's special. I don't know what to say. I've been so stuck in my own shit, I ... I didn't even think ..." He just trailed off.

"It's awright, Boss. Well, Merry Christmas. We got some more gifts to do."

The dock creaked under his weight as he walked off. Bo went inside, ashamed he was so selfish. He was mad, too. Why did Bulldog have to be so good, dammit. He knew he was mad at himself, so he turned up the rum.

CHAPTER 40

Christmas Day was bright, real bright. Church bells rang as clear and as crisp as the day. The noon plane circled overhead, putting the island on notice and setting up the approach to North Eleuthera.

Thirty minutes later, the radio in Reggie's cab crackled, "Reggie! Come roun' and fetch a passenger on the govment dock. It's dat new director fo da research centa."

"He's early. He's not s'pose to be here til nex' week, but I'll be right dare."

The bags and books and passenger were loaded.

"I'm Reggie. Nice to meet you, Director. You have come to our island early?"

"Nice to meet you. I wanted to come early to get familiar with some things, so when I officially start, I can hit the ground running."

"Dats a good thought, Director. I got instructions to take you to da villa."

"That will be okay. I need to go to the dock first, please."

"You really *do* want to get yourself started!"

"Yes. I do."

Reggie backed the van to the head of the dock at the research center.

"I take you tings to the villa, then come back to collect you, say one hour? Will that be enough time?"

"No. Thank you. This may take all afternoon, all night too."

" 'Scuse me?"

"I'll call you. Thank you very much."

Reggie watched curiously as the new director walked down the dock.

————•————

Bo sat on the covering boards looking down, just staring into nothing. No hope. Tits sat looking up, staring into Bo. Hoping.

Splat, on the deck something fell. Shit, Bo, that's not a tear, no, you've never seen your own tears. You don't have any. Probably that damn alcohol weeping from your eyes. You don't cry. It must be alcohol.

Tits' tail started to wag.

"What are you so happy about? Hell, I talk to you like you can understand. Maybe you do."

Flip Flop. Two flip-flops fell at his feet. His heart stopped, but he didn't dare look up. He was aware of the shadow cast on the deck, but still, it was a shadow of doubt. A slice of Bahamian bread softly landed next to Tits. The white bread's whiteness blinded the shadow. There was no doubt.

"Fish on," he whispered. He smiled, really smiled, for the first time in a year and a half.

"Merry Christmas, Cap'n Bo. Would you please be so kind as to tell me which one goes on which foot?"

Florida

Palm Beach

Ft. Lauderdale

Miami

Florida
Keys

Walker's Cay

LITTLE BAHAMAS BANK

Abaco Cays

Grand Bahama

Great Abaco Island

Great Isaac

Bimini
Gun Cay
Cat Cay

Berry   Islands

Harbour Island

Eleuthera Island

Nassau

New Providence

EXUMA SOUND

Cat

GREAT BAHAMA BANKS

Andros
Island

Exuma
Cays

Concep

Great Exuma

Jumentos

Ragged

Cuba

Ma